The Idols Will Fall

The Idols Will Fall

The Story of the Seven Sleepers of the Cave

Muhammad Saeed Bahmanpour

British Library Cataloguing-in-Publication Data
A catalogue record for this book is available from the
British Library.

ISBN-10: 1-904063-33-0 (pbk)
ISBN-13: 978-1-904063-33-9 (pbk)

Written in Persian by Muhammad Saeed Bahmanpour
Translated by Houri Sanizadeh
Edited by Amina Inloes

Published by
ICAS Press
133 High Road, Willesden, London NW10 2SW.
www.islamic-college.ac.uk

أصحاب الكهف

PRELUDE

T he bewildered sun rose over the brilliant blue skies of Philadelphia – not the modern namesake, but the original Philadelphia which lay, almost two thousand years ago, deep in the Middle East. Shaking off their sleep, the common folk trickled into the markets that formed the lifeblood of the city. Today fell into the rhythm of yesterday and would be echoed by tomorrow. Buying, selling, dealing, trading, as if they had no other purpose in life ... had none of them ever stopped to ponder this endless cycle?

Plutonius had. Twelve thousand days (which had given him a little over thirty years) had still not prepared him for this day, nor had languishing in this dim, dank dungeon. What was supposed to feel? Hate? Fear? Hope? His knees trembled, and yet an enigmatic peace filled his entire being.

A woman's screams shattered his brief calm, and he leapt towards the bars of his cell. Peering out, his eyes met... nothing, just like every other time he had tried to glean some news from the guts of the other cells. His mind flashed back to the night before, to the torture room.

Hoping that his screams had not given her nightmares, he edged himself back from the bars and set himself down in the least agonizing position. So much had been taken from him, but he could still see and hear. Without his eyes and ears, he wouldn't be Plutonius. *My God, is that all I am? Eyes and ears?* He wept at his insignificance. Had his life been futile?

No. His heart did not believe that, and neither did the prophet he had put his faith in.

In the path of God, he affirmed to himself. I sacrifice myself to the One in whose hand is the past and the future, who will revive the unfinished. Surely, God will accept the sacrifice of the devoted.

'Plutonius!' A rough, churlish voice summoned him.

'O Jesus, son of Mary,' he murmured.

'It's time. Come out.' The clank of the key turning in the lock of the monstrous cell door rasped in his ears.

He treaded shakily across the dank prison floors, the cold air buffeting him. It was always colder inside the prison than it was outside, as if the Mediterranean winds sent all their biting cold across the prison's gangways. His tattered clothes, ripped to ribbons by the whiplashes, scarcely protected him against the chill, and, instinctively, he wrapped his arms around his thin, lacerated body.

'No breakfast today?' the guard jibed him.

'I have no need,' Plutonius replied softly.

The guard smiled meaningfully. In an inept attempt at sympathy, he asked, 'Anything to say?'

'I have a lot to say,' Plutonius said, 'if only you would allow me.'

'Ah, don't start preaching again. I meant, any last requests?'

Plutonius did not reply. 'Move on,' the guard commanded.

As Plutonius edged along the dark gangway, the other prisoners peered anxiously after him. Friendly voices caressed his ears. 'Trust in God, young man.' 'God is with us.' 'Don't sell your soul to the world.'

'Never,' he swore, nodding his head in the dark for emphasis before disappearing up the stairs with the guard.

The filthy, broken prison stairs took an eternity to climb. At last, they reached the warden's chambers, where the prison warden and the prison chief shared a rickety desk. The warden held a weathered scroll, and the chief held a glinting pair of shackles.

'Today's unlucky man?' the warden grumbled.

'He's quieter than the other heretics we've got locked up down there,' the chief commented, 'but before he got here, he was quite a troublemaker. Public speeches and all.'

'So he shattered the Emperor's statue and got tired out,' the warden pronounced. Knocking over a beaten tin cup, he sputtered, 'Pour me a glass of some of the poison you gave him!'

'Not before the execution,' the chief chided him. Their semidrunken guffaws filled the room.

Impassive, Plutonius waited until the warden cleared his throat and announced, this time very seriously, 'He's at your service, gentlemen. Sign here.'

As the prison guard stamped his signet ring onto the warden's book, the guard removed Plutonius' handcuffs. Without allowing his swollen and bloodied wrists any repose, he shackled Plutonius' arms behind him and scowled at Plutonius' cold, dry expression. Plutonius was not going to give them a fight. He wasn't even intentionally denying them a fight. Two weeks of torture and starvation had drained the energy out of him. He had kept himself from uttering blasphemy under their duress, and that was enough. They could have his body.

Another guard appeared, and, clamping onto Plutonius' limp arms, the two dragged him out of the gaol towards the city gates, beyond which lay the stoning ditch. The sudden waft of fresh air revived Plutonius enough to realize the painful death that was imminently awaiting him.

It was early morning, an otherwise pleasant time. The streets were still empty, and they passed through them quickly. At first, a few enthusiasts followed them, until the crowd swelled to the size of a wedding party. Plutonius knew many of them had to be cursing him, but he couldn't understand their tongue. Jews and Gentiles alike traipsed after him and his guards until the crowd grew thick and impatient. All these people were here for him; all these people had gathered solely for his death. As he viewed them with the eyes of a man who had lost all hope in this world, it just all suddenly seemed so ridiculous. The din, the crowd, the gaol, the guards – everything.

He could see his destiny in the stones, clasped firmly in the hands of the onlookers. They will all follow me into the earth. Not now, but soon. Why can't they see? Frustration filled him. O world, you are so cruel! When we are with you, you mask yourself. When it's time to go, you show your face. Lucky are those who tear aside your mask and shun your countenance!

Plutonius tripped on the side of the stoning ditch, which was encircled with people and strewn with cloaks, stripped off so their owners could throw better. He knew his role. Slowly, he put his foot on the first step and began to descend.

A strong hand shoved him from behind. 'Hurry up!' Instinctively, he tried to keep balance, but to no avail. Excruciating pain shot through him as he hit the ground and lay looking upwards from his death site. Pain had become familiar to him, but barbarity had not.

'Infidel! Infidel! Unbeliever!' As the shouts crescendoed, he forced himself up. He had to get up. He didn't know why, but he did. The masses were restless. Jewish law was making them wait for the witnesses to read the testimonial of disbelief. And the government was making the witnesses wait to hear the official decree. Even though most of them weren't even Jews, they were going to pretend to do it the Jewish way today, because the Jews had been given custody of the condemned.

Finally, a guard unrolled a beaten scroll and intoned, 'Heed!' All fell silent.

'In the name of the Sovereign Emperor Hadrian,' he read methodically. 'Upon the verdict of Philadelphia's High Court…Stephanus Plutonius…originally of Rome, now of Philadelphia…on the charge of casting aspersion on the divinities…on the charge of refusing to offer sacrifice to the sacred effigy of the Emperor…on the charge of converting to the mendacious creed of Jesus of Nazareth…is hereby condemned to death.' He filled his lungs with a deep breath. 'The accused, a Jew, has been relinquished to Jewish law to be stoned under their decree.'

As the verdict was read, Plutonius surveyed the crowd. He could tell there were people there who had no idea why they had come, why they had to throw a stone. He saw Jews who had come blindly to gain the favour of Jehovah, and pagans who had come to gain the favour of Jupiter. Some were there because they were scared. Some were there to have some fun. Stoning Christians – the latest perverse form of entertainment. 'Human' didn't even seem like the right word for these wretches. But, whatever their personal reasons, they were all there to kill.

A stately man holding no stone sharply caught Plutonius' attention. Swathed in purple robes, he stood off to the side away from the rabble among the officials. Someone like him had nothing to do with a common man like Plutonius. But, in an instant, Plutonius saw in his eyes a brother, and a thousand degrees of social separation could not break this inexplicable bond. The aristocrat looked as if he were himself standing there in the middle of the ditch. But, quickly, he freed himself from the flash of Plutonius' gaze and stared at his feet, seemingly ashamed of the pleading in the victim's eyes.

Elsewhere, Plutonius caught sight of another sorrowful face. It was Judah, the man who had guided him towards Christianity and was now seeing the fruit of his efforts. Despite the unfolding travesty, he knew that Judah would never for a moment doubt the righteousness of his call, nor would he bear the slightest twinge of guilt for causing Plutonius' blood to be shed. Beside him stood Hashim, a Syrian man who had converted to Christianity after Plutonius. He looked as if he were making a great effort to block his tears, to silently say that he did not feel sad, he felt happy that Plutonius would soon be reunited with his Creator. Plutonius wept Hashim's tears for him.

The first stone struck him. 'O Jesus, son of Mary,' he whispered. Involuntarily, he sought refuge in the aristocrat's gaze. Alas, that way was closed to him, for the man's eyes were clamped shut.

The next stone cracked his brow, and blood seeped into his right eye. A larger stone landed square on his stomach, and he doubled over onto his knees, the stones raining from all sides. Shielding his body with his back, he laid his face on the ground and took sanctuary, as he spoke his last words.

'O Lord! Absolve me! Forgive me of my sins!'

Moments later, he disappeared under a mass of stones.

PART ONE

I

THE SUMMONS

Long after the rabble had dispersed, Maximilian remained fixated in place. Although he was not a sheltered man, the pitiful expression on Plutonius' face had sliced through his heart. With certain dread, he realized that he would be forced to relive the execution again and again in the coming days. He said a silent prayer.

'Sir,' the carriage driver intervened, 'oughtn't we to leave for your appointment now?'

Grimly, Maximilian turned his back to the stoning ditch and hoisted himself into the shining brass carriage, his deep indigo sash fluttering in the breeze. He had a long day ahead of him, but he was already exhausted.

Discreetly, the driver asked, 'To the palace, sir?'

'Yes,' Maximilian commanded sharply.

With a snap of the reins, the carriage rumbled off over the cobbled Philadelphian lanes. The commoners, bustling to and fro, scattered out of their path. As they sped past the grocers and the smithies and the glassblowers and the ramshackle homes, the shadow of the great amphitheatre loomed over them. A flattery of the Roman Coliseum, it was nonetheless imposing in its own right, and the Roman conquerors put it to good use. Instinctively, Maximilian shrunk back from its macabre facade.

The carriage lurched as it halted in front of the columned, ornate Temple of Jupiter. The plaza was packed, and they had to wait for the supplicants to disperse before they could carry on. *How odd*, thought Maximilian. *The temple, the amphitheatre, and the stoning ditch – they're completely different, and yet they all feel the same. What could they have in common?* He thought a bit and then, as usual, supplied his own answer, since he rarely dared to voice his thoughts aloud. *It's all in their minds – people's minds. They decide that temples are sacred, so the temples are sanctified. They decide that statues are gods, so the statues are worshipped. They decide that heretics are rebels, so the rebels –* he shivered – *are stoned.*

What makes them so blind? Their blindness brings catastrophes upon themselves. He thought some more. Whoever guides the people bears the responsibility. He shapes them like the craftsmen shape their goods. He teaches them what is and what is not, what they must and must not do. Be they godly or evil, selfless or selfish, they control the masses. Should they teach correctly, they can exalt society to great heights. But should they err, they and their peoples are doomed.

Despite the gravity of the situation, an ironic chuckle escaped his lips. Physicians bestow life to the dead, he pondered, but these men manoeuvre life itself. The physicians may be prestigious, but, in reality, they are really these wise men's slaves. So why is it that thought is traded cheaper than anything else?

Some Bible verses came to his mind. His friend Iamelichos had recited them to him in secret the night before from the Gospel of Barnabas. Of course, Maximilian himself had long since committed all these verses to memory.

How vigilant you should be in shutting Satan out from your heart, in preventing him from placing his thoughts there. For Our Lord has entrusted your heart to you, and it is the home in which He dwells.

See how a moneylender examines a coin. Has Caesar's face been properly minted? Has the silver been falsified? Is it heavy enough? He holds it in his hand and turns it over again and again. Ah, mad world... your servants are more prudent than the servants of God! Tell me, now, who scrutinizes his thoughts more than a moneylender scrutinizes a single silver coin? No one.

Damn them! Maximilian screamed from the depths of his soul, his fists clenched and sweat dripping down his face. Damn you, Jupiter, and your priests! Damn your temples and offerings! Damn Olympia and the Capitoline and Delphi and the Pantheon! As a silent rage overtook him, Plutonius' haunted gaze stared back at him. In his mind's eye, he saw Plutonius turning back to him, pleading for help, but he was helpless to do anything – even to look up. He saw solitary tears sliding from Plutonius' eyes even as Plutonius thought he had forsaken him.

'Sir,' the driver announced. Maximilian looked up. The dusty city streets had yielded to the luxurious palace gardens, from which the scent of roses and jasmine wafted towards him. Shifting weightily, he placed himself firmly in the moment. There was no room for inattention. The slightest slip could be fatal – and not only to himself. Once again, he had been called for another meeting with the local governor Diocletian, whose cruelty and villainy was well renowned. The locals called him *Daghiyanous* in their Syriac tongue, but Diocletian hardly cared. Donkeys meant more to him than the natives. But one hapless group ranked lower in his eyes than the locals, and that was the Christians. The pagans were at once repelled and amazed by the fervour with which he carried out the Emperor's command to terrorize the unfortunate Christians of Philadelphia.

But what astonished them even more was how a tyrant like Diocletian could attract such cultured and noble personalities like Maximilian to serve as his aides and his counsellors. Could they really be so blind? Or had Diocletian bought them? Or did they imagine they could use him for their own ends? No one knew which side to wager on, which side would prevail in the deadly game of royal intrigue.

Drawing himself up to his full stature, Maximilian climbed out of the carriage and ascended the smooth, wide marble palace steps. Guards stationed between sturdy, engraved columns flanked him on both sides. 'Hail,' he returned their greetings in the official tongue, although he knew that others found it quaint that someone like him would deign to reply to conscripts like them.

As the guards parted their spears, he entered the antechamber sombrely. An assemblage of counsellors and priests stared back at him.

'You are late,' Diocletian censured him. Was there a slight hint of injury in his voice?

'I beg your pardon, Excellency,' Maximilian apologized, hastily adding, 'The summons arrived early this morning. Surely, there must be a matter of great import.'

'You cannot evade me, *Maximilianos*,' Diocletian said, a knowing smile flickering on his pale face. Maximilian's heart sunk. 'I know where you were. You were watching the stoning of that *Christian*' — he spoke it like an insult — 'who, instead of prostrating before the statue of the Emperor like any decent plebeian, took it upon himself to knock it to pieces.'

'Yes, your Excellency,' voiced Maximilian. He knew Joannes was looking at him expectantly. Had he been able to do anything for the victim today? He had not. He hung his head in shame.

Diocletian drew his breath in noisily. 'Ah... I have always loved such scenes!' The animation in his eyes left Maximilian with no doubt about his sincerity. 'Especially with so much gossip going around. But I see enough blood and guts in the amphitheatre as it is.' He leaned forward furtively. 'What is it about these Christians, *Maximilianos*? You seem to understand something about them. What is it that I cannot see? They act like madmen! They throw their lives away for a god they cannot even see. You kill them, you torture them, you throw them into the sea, you toss them to the lions… and they keep multiplying. They're like vermin. They're everywhere! You name it, and they've infiltrated it – Rome, Athens, Antioch, Cyprus, Crete, Palestine, and now Philadelphia.' He lowered his voice to a whisper. 'They've even penetrated the palace.'

'How do these washermen worm their way into the palace?' Bertus interrupted, the rich brocade of his priest's robes glimmering in the dim light. 'Perhaps through the royal laundry rooms!'

He shook with laughter, and his priests quickly understood that they should follow suit. He was, after all, the second highest religious authority in Rome. And since the pontiff was always tied up in Rome on official business, Bertus held the soul of the Empire in his hands. Maximilian resisted the urge to lash out at him.

Diocletian brought them back to rapt attention. 'Recent events cannot be denied. You know what happened to Flavius Clemens and his wife.' Indeed, Maximilian did. The Emperor Domitian had poisoned them to death for apostasy – even though Flavius Clemens was his cousin – and palace rumour had not forgotten.

'How has this son-of-a-so-called-virgin pulled the

wool over their eyes? They're stupid. They're getting killed every day, and their god can't protect them. But they still keep worshipping him.' Rapping his finger for emphasis, Diocletian continued his diatribe. 'Normal people, *sane* people like you and me worship gods to get something in return. It's a business deal, just like you see in the markets. The farmers offer their sacrifices, and their crops grow. Parents drop off a few coins in the temple, and their children are cured. The pious revere their ancestral gods, and their family gods protect them from the wrath of other gods. It's quite simple, really. But it's madness to worship a god who is so weak that he cannot even protect his followers. Is it not so, Bertus?'

'Yes, Excellently,' Bertus agreed zealously. 'You speak the truth, most clear.'

'They don't even know what their god looks like. Their craftsmen can't forge a statue of him. They live in pain and misery and suffering. But forget them. Their god couldn't even defend his own prophet from a handful of Jews! Look at us, we vanquished the Jews years ago, but the Jews crucified their pathetic prophet. They're mad, they truly are, and worshipping a god like that is nothing but insanity.' Diocletian gestured upwards to an immaculate bust peering down from the dais. 'Look at the grandeur and magnificence of Apollo. Apollo, the powerful son of the mighty Jupiter... not the weakling son of an invisible god.'

Iamelichos' face was flushed. Joannes looked as if he wanted to disappear. Maximilian opened his mouth. 'I don't think it's that simple, Excellency,' he began, keeping his tone light and neutral. 'They see their God as the Lord of the Universe, the Creator of all things. They think their fate rests in His hands, both in this life and in the next. To them, He has no material form, so of course they're not going to make a statue out of Him. Indeed, they await death so they may see Him – not with their eyes, but with their hearts.'

Bertus raised a bushy eyebrow, and Iamelichos flashed Maximilian a warning gaze.

'Of course,' added Maximilian, 'that's what they say.'

The eyebrow lowered.

'Ah, yes, the Creator of the World!' Diocletian rejoined. 'Life after death! And how exactly do they know what happens after death? Did anyone ever come back and tell them? I highly doubt it.' He chuckled. 'And what about their Creator of the World? Were they there to see his Creating? These stories are old, *Maximilianos*. The tribesmen told them as they gathered around their fires to comfort themselves in the wilderness. This is Rome, the greatest civilization the world has ever known. If they have to believe in gods, let them believe in ours, for they have been eternally appointed to administer the world – whether their creator-of-the-world agrees or not.'

'Excellency,' Iamelichos interrupted. 'I do not believe such an urgent summons was sent for us to philosophize about the Christians. Should we not attend to the matter at hand?'

A momentary confusion settled across Diocletian's

face. 'Indeed,' he replied slowly. 'I sometimes need a counsellor like you to keep me focused. Otherwise, I could go on about these heretics all day.' He cleared his throat. 'As for why you have been gathered here today, I am honoured to announce that we are expecting to host a great event, and the preparations must commence today.'

'A great event, your Excellency?' one of the counsellors asked.

'Yes,' confirmed Diocletian. 'His Highness, the Emperor Hadrian, has announced that he shall honour the outlying provinces of the Empire with his auspicious presence. On his way to Jerusalem, he might stop here, in Philadelphia.'

'Might?' asked Martinos, the youngest of the counsellors.

'Might,' said Diocletian, 'as he may alter his route. But, presently, he has determined to travel this way, and we must entertain the supposition of his arrival.'

'O Powerful and Exalted Jupiter!' cried out one of Bertus' more ambitious priests. 'What a great fortune – to meet the Emperor! No, no, not the Emperor – the god of half the world! What have we done to merit such an honour?'

Both Bertus and Domitian appeared slightly bemused. Ignoring the overenthusiastic outburst, a counsellor named Julian stroked his beard. 'Most likely,' he suggested, 'His Highness the Emperor intends to visit Jerusalem to pay homage at the newly built Temple of Jupiter.'

'So far from Rome?' inquired Martinos.

'Don't forget,' replied Julian, 'it took three years to build the Temple. The Jews put up quite a fight.' From the tone of his voice, it was hard to tell how he felt about it.

Diocletian's eyes widened. 'Those ignorant Israelites! They dared to confront the power of the Empire and the might of Mars! What became of them? We crushed them. We ran our chariots and legions and cavalry and batter-rams over them until they crumpled in defeat. A wiser people would have stood aside. But they paid dearly for causing that delay.'

'Only fools would revolt against the successor to Trajan,' added a high priest bearing the emblem of Apollo. 'Under Trajan, the Roman war machines smashed the Parthian might, and Ctesiphon fell to our horses' hooves. Trajan's mammoth ships dominated the Persian sea, and the civilised world fell under the rule of Jupiter. Yes, the worshippers of Jehovah were very foolish to contend with such a man.'

Iamelichos' face was now a deep red, and he was clearly restraining himself. 'Rome's power is beyond dispute, but let not conquerors boast, let they face future defeat. Power destroys itself and makes the mighty vain. And vanity leads to defeat and robs the mighty of their power. Why is it that the mighty never reflect on their predecessors?'

He paused, sorrow etched across his face. 'What did attacking Persia do for us? All we took home from that campaign were casualties. Our ranks burgeoned with the dead and the wounded and the widows and the orphans. And, in the end, all we did was retreat from that bitter land.'

'So we retreated,' intervened Diocletian. 'But tales of Ctesiphon's conquest have deafened the world's ears. Everyone, now – even the Parthian chieftains – knows how to treat us with respect.' He indicated a faint scar on his arm. 'What do you know about war, Iamelichos? You've lived a soft life, here in the palace. You think of war in terms of casualties. But a true commander knows that life is the cheapest commodity.' He shook his head in reminiscence. 'What battles! What honours! Surely, you remember, Julian?'

'Yes, Excellency,' Julian affirmed politely.

'Where were you during the great battles over Mesopotamia?' Diocletian asked. 'I, Iamelichos, *I* commanded the entire legion. What excitement! The soldiers needed an omen, so the priests let the chickens out of their cages and strewed seeds for them all across the ground. And they ate. My god, how they ate! After that, we had no doubt that the war would go in our favour.'

He gestured animatedly. 'Thereupon, our consul took to the enemy streets and proclaimed: O ye gods! Abandon your temples and your homes! Rain down upon them sorrow and blood! Do not defend these base folk against our swords and spears. Let us enter this city victorious! We shall worship you like none of them ever did and offer you sacrifices that they never could. We will erect great temples and consecrate special servants for you as soon as we return to our fatherland. But if you resist, beware: for Apollo and Mars support us, and Jupiter reigns above them. You will never be able to fight them.' He sighed longingly. 'Ah, those were the times!'

Martinos jumped in before Diocletian could catch his breath. 'Your Excellency spoke of preparations. Might he explain what needs to be done?'

Diocletian took a moment and blinked. Composing himself, he replied, 'Yes, we must plan grand festivities for the Emperor's arrival. The city must be spotless. The amphitheatre must be worthy of the Emperor's presence. We need to lay in a good supply of gladiators and beasts in the amphitheatre's cellars. Bulls, dogs, bears, and some lions.' He chortled. 'I'm sure he'd love to see a few Christians!'

'Christians?' asked Maximilian. 'Is that really necessary?'

'Late nights have dulled your intellect, *Maximilianos*,' Diocletian replied. 'The Emperor needs his sport. He's already seen his share of catfights in the Coliseum.'

Maximilian remained silent.

'Meanwhile,' Diocletian continued, 'all the temples must be repaired. Everything must be perfect. I want a new statue of Janus, the god of the Gates, carved on the city gates. This is their responsibility, of course' – he indicated the gaggle of leechlike *flamenes* and priests – 'but you must supervise their work, give them what they need. If you need more taxes, by all means, collect them.

But don't spend too much; I still need to commission a gift worthy of the Emperor. Gods of Olympia, I still don't know what to get him.'

'Excellency!' Exakoustodianos, the financial adviser, protested. 'Those improvements hardly require new taxes!'

'True,' said Diocletian. 'But we need to offer the Emperor something worthy of his status.'

'Excellency,' Exakoustodianos persisted, 'we already have to send the army out to collect taxes as it is. We can't squeeze anything else out of these people'

'This is not Rome!' Diocletian reproached. 'You act ask if these two-legged creatures around us are human. They are not humans. They are cows, and cows need to be milked. If we don't milk them, their calves will.'

'But – ' Exakoustodianos objected.

'Enough,' Diocletian concluded firmly. 'Everything is possible with the sword. Report all progress to me. Our time is limited. I want an effigy of Augustus in all the temples – the Temple of Jupiter, the Temple of Pluto, the Temple of Cybele, the Temple of Apollo, the Temple of Mars, the Temple of Diana, even the Temple of Mithras – anything, Roman or pagan, that smacks of a god. His Highness the Emperor Hadrian is going to carry sweet memories home from Philadelphia.'

'It shall be done, Excellency,' Bertus confirmed.

Diocletian nodded to him courteously. 'Meanwhile, to celebrate this great honour, I have ordered a feast for tonight. I will see you there.' He paused. 'If there is nothing else, you may leave.'

As the counsellors filed out, Iamelichos approached Diocletian privately. 'Excellency,' he inquired, 'may I be excused this evening? An important matter has come up.'

Diocletian studied him briefly, just enough for Iamelichos to get the point. 'You do not enjoy our festivities, Iamelichos?'

'As I said,' Iamelichos demurred, 'it is an important matter.'

'Very well,' said Diocletian. 'The only thing the sword can't force a man into is merrymaking.' He offered a gracious smile that did not quite reach his eyes.

'Thank you, Excellency,' Iamelichos said and slowly made his way down the hall. He heard Julian's footsteps beside him.

'Don't be late for your important affair,' Julian murmured before disappearing into the courtyard.

Does Julian know? he wondered. He knew quite a bit about Julian. Like Iamelichos, Julian blatantly rejected the Roman superstitions. However, Julian went too far and lumped together Jesus and Homer, the Bible and the *Odyssey*. Given how vehemently he declared all prophets to be liars, Iamelichos was wary of approaching him – even though Julian was never able to offer a convincing explanation for his beliefs.

Iamelichos didn't know exactly how to categorize Julian's beliefs – if, indeed, beliefs could be categorized at all – but if he had to call him something, he would have called him an Epicurean. For Julian knew Epicurus' philosophy well and often employed his phraseology in his own speech.

So, yes, Iamelichos had Julian all figured out. But, the question was, what did Julian know about him?

II

THE CAVE

Then Jesus pronounced:

Whoever would live righteously should imitate the merchant who carefully watches over his shop, guarding it by day and locking it by night. He is intent on making profit. If he fears he will lose money, he will not sell — no, not even to his own brother.

Thus should you live. For your soul is the merchant, and your body the shop. It buys and sells the thoughts that your senses feed to your mind.

And the money is love. See, then, that with your love, you neither buy nor sell base thoughts that cannot profit you. Let your thoughts, speech, and deeds be for the love of God, for only in this love will you find refuge.

Truly, I say, many perform ablutions and pray. Many fast and give alms. Many study and preach — yet they are abominable before God. For they

cleanse their bodies but not their souls. They pray
with their tongues but not their hearts. They
abstain from meat but sate themselves with sin.
They give away what they do not need in order to
appear noble. They study so they may learn how
to speak, not how to work. They forbid others
from doing what they do themselves.

I swear by the existence of God that they do not
know Him with their hearts. For, if they knew
Him, they would love him. Since everything a
person has is a gift from God, he would spend it
all out of love for Him.

Carefully, Iamelichos closed the vellum Bible and
rested it on the table, fully conscious that he was one of
a select few to possess a copy of this rare script. It was
even more difficult to acquire than the standard Gospels
passed around in secret. One of Jesus' disciples by the
name of Barnabas had painstakingly written it to
counter the false teachings that had crept into the
hidden Christian faith.

Yes, he concurred, intention is everything. Certainly,
intentions without actions are meaningless – but the
wrong intention makes the deed useless. God will
recompense us according to our intentions, not just our
works. Bertus' grandiose façade flashed through his
mind, and, with an effort, he pushed it away. If he had
not distanced himself from the ignominies around him,
he would have long ago gone insane.

Footsteps pattered towards him, and Archimedes'
head appeared at the door. Although, by now,
Archimedes was old enough to know that he should not

disturb his father, Iamelichos did not mind, especially on a night like this. *This boy will be raised a Christian*, he swore, before joining his wife Maria for supper. She had laid out fresh loaves and dried fish and sweet clementines and honeyed drink – simple fare, but he partook of still less. He did not want to be burdened this night.

'Where is Gallus?' she asked, with some concern. Gallus, their house servant, usually took his meals with them. He had actually once been their slave, but Iamelichos had long ago given him his writ of freedom. Still, Gallus remained, as loyal as ever, bound by affection and something greater.

Iamelichos shrugged, but he had a fair idea of where Gallus was.

As he rose, Maria handed him a bulky parcel wrapped in coarse cloth. 'It's not much', she said apologetically, 'but it should last two or three days.' Iamelichos knew he would not eat even half of it, but he thanked her nonetheless.

Then, softly, he bent down and took his son's hands, miniatures of his own. 'Look after your mother,' he instructed him.

'Yes, father,' Archimedes replied.

Gently, he opened the front gate. A cool breeze and a sliver of moonlight raced in.

'Farewell,' he called, heading for the stables. There, a small tallow lamp was burning. As he had suspected, Gallus had already saddled and bridled Iamelichos' horse and was stroking its majestic mane and shoulders.

'You handle him well,' commented Iamelichos, admiring the rapport between man and horse.

'My people were master horsemen,' replied Gallus. It was not the first time they had had that conversation, but Gallus never tired of reliving the Carthaginian glory which had been shattered by the Roman conquest, after which his ancestors had been captured and sold as Roman slaves. Gallus would be the first of his line in generations to live and die as a free man.

'Many thanks,' said Iamelichos, hoisting himself onto the saddle.

Gallus watched him go. 'Pray for me, Master,' he called out in a slightly awed tone, just loud enough for Iamelichos to hear. Maria too gazed after him from the doorway of the villa he had left behind.

Brilliant torches had been lit all around the palace gardens. Hastily, Iamelichos veered off the main road. The clang of cymbals and the rattle of tambourines escaped the palace walls, and, in his mind's eye, he could see the dinnertime entertainment just warming up. He pictured the massive feast being served at the expense of the locals. At least Exakoustodianos had objected to Diocletian's insane tax plan; it just proved that – although Iamelichos firmly believed in the necessity of the message – Christians were not the only ones with basic morality.

He rode on. As he had expected, the city gates were shut tight, the night guards at their posts. Unfazed, Iamelichos made for a narrow tunnel known only to Christians, criminals and the city's elite. It wasn't as if he wanted the gatekeepers to know where he was going anyway. Before long, Philadelphia was devoid of his presence.

Although the moonlight demarcated his path, Iamelichos needed no guide, for his destination towered plainly before him. As he tirelessly rode south, the craggy slopes of Mount Angelos loomed larger and larger until, at last, he began ascending a faintly-used path winding its way to and fro around massive boulders and sheer drops. Soon, the horse could no longer find its footing, and Iamelichos had to dismount and lead it himself. Here and there, a few trees clung to the steep slopes, fed by a far-off mountain spring. Only the soft crunch of their footsteps and the sporadic twitter of night birds acknowledged their presence in this wilderness. Far off, a few stray lights still twinkled in the village of Raqim.

Deftly, he led the horse on, until, at last, they reached the untouched entrance to the cave.

The cave's entrance was fortuitously hidden within the southern slopes of Mount Angelos. Only the most astute of passer-bys would have thought it anything but another boulder. However – as Iamelichos had one day discovered – its unimposing entrance belied its enormous size. The front of the cave was flat, like a natural vestibule. Further inside, the rocks jutted upwards abruptly, creating a gigantic natural platform – as if God had willed to create a great hall. To Iamelichos, it felt absolutely perfect.

After hanging a bagful of hay from his horse's

muzzle, he let it be. Of course, the horse did not stray far. Then he set himself down on the damp ground to rest a bit and prepared himself for what he had come for.

By now, all of Raqim was sound asleep – except one young man. With the surefootedness of a shepherd, Antonios scrambled up the familiar slopes of Mount Angelos. While the average villager might have had more sense than to tread such a treacherous path, Antonios leapt from rocky patch to rocky patch as if he were retracing the route to his home, for this path led to his own special cave – the cave in which he often sought solace for prayers and solitude.

What was it about this nondescript cave nestled in the heart of this great mountain? Why not simply commune with his Lord at home?

Perhaps the towering mountain inspired him with a sense of his own humility. Perhaps the expansive view reminded him that he was not the centre of the world. Perhaps secluding himself gave him occasion for reflection and made him ready to worship its Creator.

Or perhaps it was something else.

At any rate, Antonios lost no time in reaching the pleasantly secretive entrance to his cave. But, suddenly, he stopped dead in his tracks. An otherworldly sound in the dead of night whispered into his ears. Quietly, he kneeled, so as not to interrupt it, and craned his neck. It was as if the cave was weeping.

I have erred so much, but my errors pale before

your compassion. You are too exalted to take me to account for all my deeds. You act as you are — merciful and great — and I act as I am, lowly and abased.

You have given me everything, even though everything you gave me was nothing to you. In a moment, you can do what I can never. My life and death, my misery and happiness all rest in your hands. You could easily dismiss me, but I could never live without you.

You created me and sustained me. You guided me and sheltered me. You pardoned me and forgave me. When I tired of the robes of servility, you clothed me in honour. Even after I disobeyed you, you still inspired others to praise me.

What did I do then? I took advantage of your generosity and asked you for more than I deserve. And you let me do this! Why? Because you wanted me to approach you in familiarity, not in fear. You *wanted* me to ask you for whatever I wished.

I became arrogant. I lost patience when you denied me my requests — even though you held them back for my own good. For you know the end of all things, and I do not.

Still, you come towards me, but I back away. You befriend me, but I ignore you — as if I am better than you! How patient you are with your lowly servant! How can I face you after this?

Nevertheless, you have never ceased your mercy towards me, not even for a moment, as if I were someone who had never committed a sin… as if I were not your slave, but your friend!

Antonios could no longer distinguish the words from the sobs He too began shedding tears. Before long, the cave's weeping subsided, and he heard the voice again, imploring:

> And what have I done in return? I have been an ungrateful servant. I sold you to my whims. I exchanged your remembrance for worldly thoughts. I emboldened myself before you – as if you were obliged to me, as if you did not create me, as if you did not sustain me. And I did all this while acknowledging your blessings, eating your food, and using your bounties.

> Should you reprimand me, I deserve nothing but your wrath. But your mercy defies imagination! Neither does your servants' rebellion harm you, nor does their obedience aid you. So, I beseech you, my Creator, overlook my stumbling. Do not treat me according to my deeds. Do not let my sins cease your mercy, or I will perish, for nothing can save me except your grace. Only your love can lift me from my poverty.

Magnified in the darkness, Antonios heard the familiar sound of a horse chomping its bit. Straining his eyes, he barely made out the shape of a noble Arabian steed. He heard weeping again, and then silence. Then, some astonishing words came forth and caressed his pained ears:

> O God, your servants, the followers of Jesus, are suffering at the hands of the most vicious men. The roar of tyranny has deafened the world. Deviation has penetrated our faith. God, when will you lift us from this despotism and ignorance

which has rooted itself in people's beings? Yes, we do not deserve your mercy, but you have always bestowed your mercy upon us nonetheless.

And then Antonios heard some words he did not understand.

You will shine your strongest light on Mount Paran, even more luminously than you did on Mount Seir, and even more gloriously than you did on Mount Horeb.

The names became more recognizable.

O Lord, answer Abraham's prayers. Bring about Jesus' glad tidings. We have been awaiting him for a long time. We may not be worthy of him now, but you can make us worthy of his advent. O Creator, through your grace —

Antonios could contain himself no more. Swallowing hard, he wiped his cheeks with the back of his rough hands. Then, clearing his throat, he called out, 'Christian brother!' His voice echoed off the rock stifled and hoarse, not his own. There was no reply. He tried again. 'Christian brother! Christian brother!'

Doubt suddenly seeped into him. 'Christian brother?'

III

ANTONIOS

Iamelichos froze, his head half raised from the ground, still on his knees. He had never thought about what to do if someone came along. Involuntarily, he turned around. At the entrance, the moonlight shone on a young man in shepherd's clothes. 'Christian brother!' he called out. 'Christian brother?'

'Who is there?' Iamelichos demanded, learned dread flooding through him.

'One of the faithful,' the youth answered, 'your brethren.'

Iamelichos relaxed a bit. 'How do you know me?'

'How do I know you?' he exclaimed. 'I was praying alongside you. How beautifully you pray! Who are you? A teacher of the Gospel? No, you pray like a saint!' He scrutinized Iamelichos. 'You look like you're from the city. Where are you from? How did you find this cave?'

'Now that we are brothers,' said Iamelichos, 'what difference does it make?'

35

'Your robes are those of a courtier,' the young man continued, 'but your words are those of a saint. You are of nobility, no?'

'Are you not a Christian?' Iamelichos reprimanded.

'I certainly am,' he affirmed.

'Then why speak like the unbelievers? Rich or poor, high or low, townsman or countryman – these are false divisions. They mean nothing in the face of Truth. Knowledge and piety, now, those are real matters. God will judge a man on his knowledge or his piety. But God does not care if you are an aristocrat or a plebeian. You shouldn't judge people on artificial values. Wealth does not make an ignoble person great, nor does poverty abase the noble – even though it may seem to.'

'I do not understand most of what you are saying,' commented the youth, 'but you seem very educated.'

'Brother, what is your name?'

'Antonios.'

'They do not use the name *Antonios* here. Are you from Rome?'

'Kind of. My ancestors tilled the earth there. But the Romans started bringing in more and more slaves to work the land, and we were forced out. My father left Rome in search of a better life. I don't know how, or why, but he ended up here. Alas, our situation did not improve, and I now shepherd other people's sheep.'

'So, you have left farming,' Iamelichos observed.

'No,' Antonios said. 'We have a small plot of land here. But with the taxes like this, there's no way we could survive on what it grows.'

A pained expression crossed Iamelichos' face. 'Yes,' concurred Antonios, 'they are very cruel. But I always thank God that I do not treat anyone that way. They say that being an oppressor is as bad as being oppressed. But I think being an oppressor is far worse. You can't control what people do to you, but you can control what you do to them. People only oppress others by choice.'

Iamelichos nodded in agreement. 'Well,' Antonios asked, 'what's your name?'

'Iamelichos.'

'Iamelichos, Iamelichos...where have I heard that name before? In the city, perhaps?'

'Do you come to the city often?' Iamelichos interceded, trying to distract him.

'No, only now and then. Once in a while, I make the pilgrimage to the shrine of Prophet Uria so that people think I'm a Jew and I can come and go freely.' He kept thinking. 'Iamelichos, Iamelichos....'

'How did you convert to Christianity?'

'I didn't convert. I was born a Christian. My father converted in Trajan's time, before the Emperor ordered the persecution of Christians. I'm sure you know about that. Fortunately, I had the honour of being born to a Christian mother and a Christian father.' Suddenly, he paused. 'Iamelichos! I knew I'd heard that name somewhere before. Oh my God, Iamelichos!' Ever so slightly, he shrunk back. 'Iamelichos works for Diocletian!'

'So,' said Iamelichos indifferently, 'what does that

have to do with me?'

'Nothing,' Antonios concluded. 'What a silly notion. Diocletian's counsellor, the Christians' enemy.' He smiled ruefully. 'There is no way you could be *that* Iamelichos. But, you know, you're dressed like him. Very nicely. Say, you never told me how you found this cave, or why you come here for prayers.'

'It's a long story,' said Iamelichos, 'and now is not the time to tell it. Should I see you again, I will tell you.'

'I am very eager to meet you again,' said Antonios. 'Your prayers have really enchanted me. Where did you learn them?' Iamelichos smiled. 'I didn't understand everything you said. The Light of Seir and Horeb and all. And who were you talking about? The Messiah who Jesus promised would come?'

Iamelichos deliberated for a few moments, examining Antonio's face. It was wide with enthusiasm and innocence. Finally, he inquired, 'Have you read the Holy Book?'

'No, I can't read. But I've heard a lot of it and learnt some verses by heart. Actually, I do know what Seir and Horeb are. Mount Seir is where the Almighty shone his light on Jesus, and Mount Horeb is where God spoke to Moses, right?'

'It is said in Deuteronomy:

> This is the blessing that Moses, the man of God, pronounced to the Israelites before his death. He said: The Lord came from Sinai and rose up from Seir. He shone forth from Mount Paran.

The light shining from Mount Paran is the one

whom our Lord Jesus promised us, and his name is 'the praised'. Do you know where Paran is?'

'No,' said Antonios.

'Paran is the valley where Abraham housed Hagar and their son Ishmael. The praised one, the descendant of Ishmael, will arise there. I wish I could go and live there like some Jews have done.'

Antonios stared at him, amazed. His glittering eyes reflected his eagerness for Iamelichos to continue. Finally he asked, 'Brother, what is your profession?'

'Talking,' Iamelichos replied, patting Antonios on the back. What else could he tell this sincere youth? 'Well,' he added quickly, to prevent Antonios from asking any more questions, 'it's almost dawn. We had better do what we came such a long way for.'

He could tell that Antonios desperately wanted to hear more but was intimidated by Iamelichos' imposing presence. Iamelichos was thankful for that. Then, they kneeled together and began to praise their Lord.

IV

THE MEETING

L ike its neighbour Raqim, Philadelphia appeared
fast asleep. Only the sentinels ambled through the
city quarters, their torches gleaming over the moonlight,
yawning as they ignored the false alarms of stray dogs
and cats scouring the alleys for food.

But beneath the seeming calm bubbled an
undercurrent of activity. Concealed from the roving eyes
of the guards, a steady stream of the initiated tiptoed
outside the city gates towards the ancient cemetery
which lay next to the main thoroughfare that Iamelichos
had traversed hours ago.

As they crept silently beneath the pre-dawn sky,
Joannes hesitated, Diocletian's image looming large in
his mind. Was he really pleasing his Lord by gratifying
his religious feelings like this? Maybe he should just
avoid Christian society altogether — as he had done
before — and pray alone rather than risk being revealed.

The thought of seeing his friend Judah swung the

balance, and, donning his aristocrat's robes, he hastened through the still city. Then, after passing through the graveyard's rickety gates and nodding to a lone brother standing watch, he descended the broad stone hewn stairs into the lower crypts.

There, sheltered from the outside world, a small crowd of Christians had already gathered. Seated on the cold stone floor, they eagerly awaited Judah's sermon. Inconspicuously, Joannes hung at the edge of the crowd and watched Judah approach. At first, Judah's ragged face and small stature rendered him nondescript. But few dared to look into his damp yet radiant and grave eyes. Soon, the audience fell under the thrall of his exalted soul.

'Jesus said: *I have no home.* So his disciples said: *O teacher of goodness! Should we not build you a home so you can live in comfort?* Jesus took them to the shores.' He indicated the shores with his hands, and each and every listener could picture the sand and the sea, whether they had been there or not. 'Then he told them: *If you can, build me a dwelling upon the waves.* The disciples said: *Pious master! How can we build a house upon the waves? How could we make its foundations stable?* Then Jesus faced them and said: *Understand that, whatever you build in this world, its foundations are built upon these waves, and it will soon collapse.*'

As Judah's voice echoed off the stone walls, Judah caught Joannes' eye briefly with his luminous gaze, and a strong sense of familiarity flowed between them. Long-time friends, Joannes had led Judah back to his faith after he had started teaching that Jesus was the son of God. In their hours together, Joannes had also taught him great secrets of the spirit and the heart. Judah had nothing but respect for Joannes who, through his subtle, cunning influence at Diocletian's court, had liberated many of the faithful from the claws of death.

Judah resumed his sermon. 'And Jesus said: *Beware, for the world is a bridge that leads you to eternity. Simply cross over it, and do not preoccupy yourself with it.* Do you know what our Lord Jesus said when he passed a house whose owners had died, and others had moved into it?'

'No,' a man replied innocuously.

'He said,' answered Judah, 'Pity your owners who have inherited you. How were they not warned by the previous owners' fate? Yes, this is how you should regard this world.'

Judah paused, allowing his words to sink in. Through the narrow passageways, the vague twitters of birds filtered in, hinting at the slowly dawning morning light.

A swarthy man rose. 'Master, tell us how to pray to the God of Jesus. How can we pray so we are answered like the worshippers of Jupiter?'

'The God of Jesus is not a god among other gods,' Judah patiently explained. 'He is the One and only God. The God of Jesus is everyone's God. He is your God and the God of the Earth and the skies. He created everything. Anyone who calls upon any other god calls out in futility. He sustains all those who worship Jupiter and Apollo and the other false deities.

'Why would he do that?' asked a peasant woman, seated near Joannes.

'Out of love,' replied Judah. 'He gives them so much, though, that the ignorant have come to believe that Jupiter or Mithras has answered them. Can Jupiter or Mithras hear? Of course not. Even if they could hear, they could not reply. So only call upon Him, for only He can respond.

'Fear God! Do not depict Him in your image as the pagans have done. He is nothing like you. Fear no one but Him, and ponder no god but Him. He has not delegated His authority to other deities. He holds all His power in His own grasp. He confers no affair to others – not even the slightest – and He controls all things. Call upon Him alone, and you will see. He will speedily reply'

'Then why doesn't He reply?' the man persisted in the torch lit darkness. 'We call upon Him every day. Why doesn't He answer?' A few murmurs passed through the crowd.

Judah turned his intense gaze on the questioner. 'Do not call upon Him as you call upon Venus and Jupiter and Mithras and Isis. God told Jesus: *O Jesus! Warn the Israelite oppressors not to call upon me with stolen goods in their arms and idols in their homes. For I have sworn to answer all that call upon me, but my answer to them will be nothing but damnation.*'

He continued, now in full force. 'Call upon him with a pure heart and mind cleansed of belief in other gods.

Call upon Him with an untainted tongue and praiseworthy deeds. For God has said to Jesus: *O Jesus! Purify your body with water, but purify your soul with good deeds, for you will soon return to me. Seek not enlightenment while in sin or amusement. Detach yourself from deadly lusts, and distance yourself from desires that might distance you from me. Know that your rank with me is that of a faithful prophet, so beware. Know that your world will eventually lead you to me, and, in my wisdom, I shall receive you. So when you remember me, debase your ego and fill your heart with humility and fear. Be wakeful while the negligent sleep.'*

In a softer tone, he concluded, 'Do you now understand how to call upon Him?'

'I do,' acknowledged the man. Out of the corner of his eye, Joannes noticed one of the worshippers disappear up the stairs, but he paid him no heed.

The peasant woman raised her voice again. 'O Teacher, why should we worship God when He has no need of our offerings?'

'Indeed!' agreed another.

'Know, woman,' replied Judah, 'that the prophets have come to unite us with God. But I swear on the soul of my Lord Jesus that this union does nothing for God. It only benefits His servants. Nothing ascends from this world but evil, and nothing descends from Him but good. This union requires a medium, and that medium is worship. Worship brings you closer to goodness. A farmer who does not sow seeds waits in vain for the harvest. A person who does not worship dreams in vain of attaining perfection.

'O teacher!' another listener interrupted him. 'How can we avoid acting like the people who are in love with this world? How can we make sure we are not hypocrites?'

Judah thought momentarily. 'Remember death, and do not be enamoured by this world or by those who worship transitory joys. As God said to Jesus: *O Jesus, take heed that a bad friend befouls, and a bad companion destroys. So be mindful of whose company you keep, and choose believers as brothers.* O ye faithful! Shed tears aplenty for your sins. Know that our Lord Jesus has said: *A sinner must shed tears like a father at his son's deathbed. Insane is he who weeps over a body whose soul has left but does not shed a tear over a soul that has lost God's blessing through sin. Tell me, when a storm has wrecked a ship, what would the captain do if he could retrieve his loss through his tears? He would certainly weep, and weep hard. But I tell you the truth when I say that humans are mistaken when they cry for anything but their sins.* Indeed, man can retrieve what he has lost through ugly deeds by weeping. It is a pity that he does not choose to do so. It is a wonder that he laughs but does not cry!

'I cry,' murmured another. Looking over, Joannes recognized Hashim, one of their long-standing brethren who had been witness to many, many executions. But he was not going to dwell on that now. Hashim signalled Judah courteously, and Judah nodded. 'How should we treat our brothers?' Joannes had a feeling that Hashim was not asking for his own self.

Judah smiled. 'What you do not wish them to do unto you, do not do unto them. Should one of them slap your right cheek, turn the other cheek. Do not punish evil with evil, for this is how the worst animals act. Rather, recompense evil with good, and pray for those who have mistreated you. Fire is not put out with fire. Fire is put out with water. Know that the apostles asked Jesus: *O worthy teacher! What is the weightiest matter?* Jesus replied: *God's wrath.* They asked: *What causes God's wrath?* He replied: *Your wrath.* So they asked: *O Teacher, what inspires God's wrath in us?* He told them: *Vanity, despotism, and contempt.* Know, brother, that God told Jesus: *O Jesus, be kind and affectionate. Treat other creatures of God as you would wish them to treat you. O Jesus! Be courteous towards the weak and humble towards the beneficent. Act as they do.*'

Judah's words seemed strange to the newcomers whose minds were still tainted with paganism. Love for the worshipped was foreign to them. They saw prayer merely as a means of give and take, and their behaviour had been shaped by the customs of the day. But since they had committed to becoming believers, they memorized his every word.

The Jewish converts, on the other hand, had not worshipped the many gods of the Romans. In that regard, they were far ahead. But their hearts were as rigid as the pagans', and they too viewed prayer like a deal in the marketplace.

Another man stood. 'O Teacher, tell us – '

Shouting from outside interrupted him. The man who had been standing guard at the graveyard gates came running in. 'The soldiers!' he cried breathlessly. 'The soldiers! The soldiers! Get out of here!'

The crowd burst into confusion, with people running everywhere. Most pushed their way up the narrow stairs connecting the crypts to the outer world. Judah and Joannes locked eyes. Both knew that the soldiers would first block all avenues of escape.

Joannes rushed to Judah and grasped his hand. 'God be with you,' he prayed.

'God be with you,' invoked Judah. 'I am more worried about you.'

'I'll be fine,' swore Joannes stoically.

Seeing no other option, Joannes sped towards the passage from which he had entered. Just then, an uproar arose as the fleeing worshippers fell back, spurred on by a contingent of soldiers with drawn swords.

Suddenly, the soldiers around Joannes came to a dead halt. 'Hold your ground!' one of them yelled. Another seized Joannes' hands. Judah averted his gaze. The panicked crowd fell silent.

Joannes centred himself. *In the name of God*, he silently implored. Then he let out a roar. 'Incapable lot! Let go of my hands! Do I look like one of them? Where is your commander?' He wheeled on the soldier, his aristocrat's robes flashing through the air. 'I said, where is your commander? Can you hear me?'

The soldier stared at him wretchedly, his mouth gaping, until Syracus, the commander, stepped up from behind. Joannes and Syracus recognized each other immediately. Joannes had seen him many times at ceremonial occasions at Diocletian's court.

'Idiot!' Syracus yelled. 'What are you doing? Do you know who that is?'

The soldiers stood aghast. The crowd, with no means of escape, watched, riveted.

'It's about time!' Joannes thundered, before the commander could open his mouth. 'Was I supposed to get here before you? I sent the message hours ago! They were almost through. If they had escaped, your necks would have been cut. All of them!'

'Sir!' Syracus quavered. 'Our informant only told us about this meeting several minutes ago. Your messenger never brought us word.'

'Oh really?' growled Joannes. 'So what happened to him?'

'Excellency, believe me,' pleaded Syracus. 'I'm telling you the truth. Maybe something did happen to him. I swear by the Emperor's soul, your messenger never reached us.'

'I assure you that I will find out exactly what happened,' threatened Joannes. 'At least you got here before the party ended.'

'Forgive this soldier's discourtesy,' continued Syracus. 'I shall punish him myself.'

'No need,' allowed Joannes nobly. 'It's the messenger's fault, not his. Now take them away.'

The soldiers began tying up the worshippers' hands. Suddenly, one of them yelled out, 'Hey! Sir! It's Judah, the missionary!'

'Judah the missionary?' the commander repeated. 'What a catch!' He walked over to check it out himself. 'Treat him well. He'll fetch us a fine reward.'

The soldiers, who knew how to treat people well, bound Judah's hands, threw a rope around his neck, and pulled hard.

Relieved, Syracus turned to Joannes. 'Excellency, were you aware that Judah would be here?'

'Why do you think I came personally?' Joannes demanded. Some of the soldiers shifted uneasily.

Syracus lowered his voice. 'Certainly, you are right to be cautious,' he confided. 'I won't pretend that the arrested have never bought their freedom with a few *denarius* – or even *sestertius*. But, Excellency, you can rest assured of our integrity.'

With effort, Joannes cast him an indifferent glance. Meanwhile, Judah was dragged past them, a slight smile playing on his lips. The crypt was rapidly being emptied. Swallowing his emotions, Joannes nodded his head approvingly as they hauled Judah up the stairs. Then he beheld the Christian lot. Men, women, and even a few children stood surrounded, their hands in ropes and chains. 'Madmen!' he declared.

But Syracus had no idea whom he really meant.

V

THE TRIAL

A s soon as the soldiers had dispersed, Joannes made straight for Maximilian's house and pounded on the door with all his might. It was barely sunrise.

After seemingly ages, an aged servant opened the broad wooden door, grumbling about it being bright and early. However, as soon as he recognized Joannes, he immediately deferred to him.

'Is Excellency *Maximilianos* sleeping?' Joannes besieged him.

'No, Excellency Joannes,' replied the servant. 'He is reading.'

'Tell him Joannes is here.' The words rushed out of his mouth.

Unquestioningly, the servant led him into the tiled entrance hall and walked towards Maximilian's private library – rare among city aristocrats, who had the desire neither to read nor to pay for books – while Joannes paced impatiently, a colourful mosaic at his feet. Any other day, he might have joined Maximilian for a bit of literary rivalry, for Maximilian's library — impressive as it was — was hardly a match for his. But not today.

'Excellency *Maximilianos!*' The servant's voice drifted down the hall. 'His Excellency Joannes has arrived.'

'Send him in,' Maximilian directed. Without waiting any longer, Joannes bolted for the library.

Maximilian rose. 'Greetings, Joannes,' he acknowledged warmly, extending his hand. 'Good morning.'

'Greetings,' replied Joannes, perfunctorily shaking Maximilian's hand.

Maximilian turned towards the servant. 'Isaac!'

'Yes, Excellency?'

'Bring us two cups of *calda* to warm up our guest. It's quite chilly this morning.'

As the servant disappeared, Maximilian examined the face of his long-time friend carefully. 'What happened?' he inquired softly.

'It's Judah,' whispered Joannes.

Maximilian cast his eyes down at the Book of Solomon, lying half open on the table. 'You don't mean — '

'They caught Judah,' Joannes blurted out, shaking. Unable to support himself, he sank onto one of the library's ornate benches.

Slowly, the smile fell from Maximilian's face. His lips gradually shrank, and his brow dropped. Finally, a soft sound spilled from his lips. 'Judah? How?' His voice grew rougher, almost accusatory. 'How do you know?'

'I – ' stammered Joannes, 'I – I was there.'

'Where?'

'The dawn prayer services.'

Maximilian rounded on him. 'What were you doing *there*?'

'Never mind,' muttered Joannes. 'They took him. There was an informant in the crowd. I saw him, but I didn't....' He started shaking again. Maximilian clasped his hand firmly, his other hand resting on the Bible, as if for comfort. 'I – I didn't think. If only I had known....'

'What happened?' pressed Maximilian.

'The soldiers,' continued Joannes, reliving the event. 'They blocked off all the exits. No one could escape. They took them all.'

'*Maybe some Christians*,' murmured Maximilian. '*The Emperor needs his sport.*' Joannes stared at him, bewildered. 'Diocletian's words.' He slammed his fist down onto the table. 'How did you escape?'

Joannes shook his head. 'Don't ask. I would have gladly given my life for his.'

'Instead,' snapped Maximilian, 'he is in jail, and we are the ones who live in comfort.' He rose and walked across the library as, mutely, the servant entered and set down two steaming terra cotta cups, a spicy aroma wafting from them. The *calda* remained untouched.

'Go see the judge,' urged Joannes. 'He's your friend. You were able to get through to him before. You can do it again.'

'Joannes!' Maximilian rebuked him. 'We're not talking about a petty thief. This is Judah – Judah, their prize! Thousands of *denarius* wouldn't even buy his freedom, and you want me to ask the judge to let him off for free? I can't keep going down to the courthouse. The judge is going to start asking me why I care so much about his convicts – and why only the Christians.' He shook his head. 'If arousing the suspicion of the judge would set Judah free, I'd go now. But there's no way they'll let go of him.'

'What else can we do?' pleaded Joannes.

Maximilian stared off into space at something invisible. 'All right,' he finally conceded. 'When is his trial?'

Joannes considered it. 'They won't try him today. Tomorrow is a state holiday. Maybe Monday, Tuesday at the latest. They can't keep him too long. They can't afford to keep the prisoners these days. The prisons are too crowded; they don't have the money to feed them.'

'Find out the exact date and time of his trial,' instructed Maximilian.

'Then what?' asked Joannes.

'I will see the judge about some important business,' promised Maximilian.

'About what?'

'Some important business that I have yet to invent. Then, I will do whatever is within my power to help him.'

'Have hope,' urged Joannes. Suddenly exhausted, he rested his face in his hands. 'God be with you.'

'God be with us all,' replied Maximilian, with much less optimism.

'Your Honour!' called out the court speaker, a perceptible Syriac accent flavouring his voice. 'The accused are ready.'

'Hold on, Qassem!' reprimanded the judge, ignoring Qassem's effusive apologies.

For the past half hour, Maximilian had been striking up a casual conversation with Judge Gaius, to no avail. Any major cases lately? Judah's trial. Certainly, rabble-rousers like him didn't deserve to live. Citizens were executed for far less. But he hadn't actually killed anyone or stolen anything. He didn't even owe any taxes. All he did was talk. So what if a few of the riffraff followed him? Half of them were petty criminals anyway, or were past due on their own taxes. Sane, purebred Romans had nothing to do with him.

Yes, of course, he was guilty. Still, maybe killing him wasn't the best idea. No need to give the masses another reason to revolt; riots had been cropping up in the frontier towns. True, stoning heretics amused the masses – for now. But be careful not to push them too far. Judah was their kinsman, after all. Why risk invoking sympathy for the Christians?

'As usual, your wits outmatch mine,' conceded the judge. 'Nevertheless, Philadelphia will be better off without him. I'm honoured to be able to convict him in my own courtroom, and I don't intend to show him any mercy. In fact, I fully intend to make an example out of him.'

'Sorry for taking up your time,' apologized Maximilian, despondently.

'No apologies necessary,' reassured the judge. 'Your counsel is always welcome.'

'With your permission,' suggested Maximilian carefully, 'I'd like to stay for the trials today, keep myself abreast of local affairs.'

'Ah, *Maximilianos*,' commended the judge. 'You do not need to ask. Despite our rather frequent differences of opinion, I have nothing but admiration for your dedication to overseeing affairs of state. Of course you may stay. I am happy to have you here.'

As Maximilian settled himself into the seats reserved for dignitaries, the judge hollered, 'Qassem! How many cases do we have today?'

'Your Honour, one debtor, two thieves, and five Christians.'

Only five, thought Maximilian. What happened to the rest?

'The thieves first, then the debtor,' dictated the judge. 'Save the Christians for last.'

After the thieves' two very short trials ended in two very heavy sentences, the guards escorted two more olive-skinned contenders in.

'Your Honour,' announced Qassem, 'the accused, Adnan Shokat' – he indicated a lean man with a sun-ripened complexion – 'is charged with defaulting on a debt of twenty-six *denarius* and three *sestertius*, due in October.'

The judge eyed the other man, who was fleshy and soft of hand. 'Are you the plaintiff?'

'No, sir,' he replied smoothly. 'I am his attorney.'

'Why could the plaintiff not come himself?' demanded the judge.

'He had other affairs to attend to,' replied the attorney.

'I see,' commented the judge. 'The honourable plaintiff's name?'

'Ma'adh Saleh. The honourable Ma'adh Saleh.'

'In that case, Saleh's attorney, let us begin.' He faced the accused. 'Do you deny the charge?'

Adnan stared at him blankly, clearly not understanding Latin. Quickly, Qassem translated the judge's question into the local tongue. Adnan spoke at length in Syriac before Qassem translated his plea.

'Your Honour, it is not my fault. Two years ago, I rented a plot of land from the honourable Ma'adh Saleh. But the harvest was poor, and I could not pay my expenses. So I borrowed twenty *denarius* from him in hopes of paying him back this year. However, this year's harvest was even worse than the last. I could not pay the rent and the taxes. I could not even buy food for my family.'

'It is not the landowner's fault either,' snapped the judge. 'He didn't force you to borrow money from him. He also has to pay his taxes. If he doesn't pay his taxes, he'll be in here too. Do you know what happens to you if you don't pay?'

Adnan hung his head. 'Your Honour,' he pleaded at

last, 'I have nothing. Tell me how I can pay?'

'You admit you are guilty,' pronounced the judge. 'Therefore, as of today, you are no longer a free man. The court hereby decrees you to be in the servitude of the honourable... the honourable – '

'Saleh,' the attorney quickly reminded him. 'The honourable Ma'adh Saleh.'

'Correct, Ma'adh Saleh,' confirmed the judge, mispronouncing the name. 'However, the court finds the amount of the debt inconsequential. Therefore, it exempts your dependents from the sentence.'

'Your Honour!' protested the attorney, as Qassem translated the bittersweet news. 'The law clearly states that the debtor's immediate family goes into the service of the lender – '

'Dismissed,' barked the judge. Mutely, Adnan and the attorney vacated the courtroom.

More law, less justice, thought Maximilian. *Summum ius, summa iniuria.* 'Wait!' he called out. Adnan looked back, curious about the exchange.

'Yes, *Maximilianos*?' inquired the judge.

'This man's debt is but *sestertius* to me. I will pay it.'

Judge Gaius smiled narrowly. 'Save your pity for the citizens. These villagers live like animals.' Qassem declined to translate that part of the speech. 'Besides, the law is the law. Once given, the verdict cannot be changed.'

With such a judge, how can justice rule the people? Maximilian felt powerless. Twice in one day, he had failed, despite his position. Anyway, even if he had liberated Adnan, what about the thousands of others like him? Something drastic needed to change.

'Next case,' commanded the judge. Immediately, Maximilian sat alert, Adnan forgotten.

A decorated military official sauntered into the room, followed by a small entourage. This was no ordinary trial. Roughly, the guards shoved three battered men and one battered woman into the courtroom. Lashes and scalding rods had branded their bare skin, and all were doubled over. One more jostle might have sent them crumbling to pieces.

Tears filled Maximilian's eyes. Just then, Judah was dragged in, a rope around his neck. The skin around the rope was rubbed raw, and blood trickled down his torso. Burn marks competed with lash marks on his exposed shoulders, which ran yellow with pus. Obviously tortured more than the others, he stumbled and fell, seemingly indifferent to the officialdom.

Just then, he caught sight of Maximilian. Ease washed over his injured face.

'Get up,' a guard demanded, kicking him. Weakly, Judah rose to his legs. He and Maximilian stared at each other wordlessly.

'Your Honour,' Qassem announced – purely as a matter of form, for everyone knew who Judah was – 'the Philadelphian guard apprehended these criminals in the cemetery on Saturday shortly after dawn as they were conducting their illegal rituals. Fifty-one were arrested, but forty-six paid obsequies to the Emperor and the gods and were released.'

The bloodied faces of the captives left no doubt about their decision. 'However,' continued Qassem needlessly, 'these five have elected not to repent. They are hereby charged with disrespecting the Emperor, insulting the state religion, and engaging in outlawed practices.'

'Outlawed, revolting practices,' boomed the officer. 'I conducted their arrest myself, your Honour, and will bear witness.'

'In that case, you may present the accosted,' said the judge.

The officer tugged on the rope binding Judah. 'I present to your court their main instigator. He has been wanted for years, and, by the grace of the gods, has finally been caught. Not only has he been caught, but he has been caught in the act. I present to you the Christian heretic, Judah.'

Was it pride that flickered across Judah's tortured face? *I should be standing up there with him*, thought Maximilian, almost envious.

Judge Gaius began with the four Christians. 'The court is willing to be lenient. End this lunacy, and save your lives.'

None of them responded – if, indeed, any had the strength to speak. 'Where are they from?' asked the judge.

'This one is a Roman citizen,' answered the officer, pointing to a man. 'The lady is a Jewess.'

'A Philadelphian Jew?'

'No, from Baalbek. But the other two are

Philadelphians.'

'Jews?' inquired the judge.

'No,' replied the officer. 'Citizens.'

'Philadelphian citizens,' echoed the judge, bending his head over a book of law, although he did not appear to be reading. 'So be it. The accused have rejected the opportunity to recant their offence. Therefore, their verdict is death.'

The woman began sobbing in Aramaic, something about an infant. Maximilian wanted to scream, but the scream froze, stifled in his throat.

'The Roman is to be decapitated,' continued the judge. 'Release the Jew to the Jews so they can stone her according to their own laws.'

All Maximilian could think of was Plutonius, sinking beneath the mountain of stones. He shuddered, and his stomach heaved. Closing his eyes, he clenched his fist and tried to focus on anything else.

'As for the Philadelphians,' the judge concluded reluctantly, 'the imperial decree is clear.' He was still looking down. 'Bind their hands, and throw them to the lions in the amphitheatre.'

The court was absolutely silent. Attention turned to Judah. 'You,' the judge accused, meeting him squarely in the eye. 'I hold you accountable for this. You have misled enough innocents. There is no question you will die. However, the law offers you one last mercy. Repent, and you will die faster.'

Despite his injuries, Judah pulled himself up. 'Your Honour, you are asking us to free ourselves? We are already free. You are the ones who are enslaved.' His voice strengthened. 'Free yourselves! Liberate yourselves from the shackles of your lusts and desires. Liberate yourselves from the gods you have wrought with your own hands.'

The courtroom watched in awe. 'Look at him,' one of the guards whispered. 'He can still talk.'

'Are we crazy?' continued Judah, ignoring the blood, ignoring his wounds. 'We follow reason. We follow the truth. No, we are not crazy. You are the ones who are insane! You have sold your souls to imaginary deities. We follow the prophet of God. You follow gods without prophets. We pray to a powerful God who can answer our prayers. You pray to iron and stone. Tell me, now, who are the real madmen?'

'Their lunacy knows no end,' observed the judge.

Unable to sit still anymore, Maximilian leapt to his feet. Slowly, he approached Judah and circled him with measured steps, all the while examining him very carefully. Then, in a last bid, he addressed the court. 'Indeed, your Honour, they have been afflicted with insanity. They are completely senseless!' He feigned slapping one of the Christians as the others watched on with dread. 'They feel no pain. They could buy their freedom with a single word, but they choose torment instead. I see no explanation other than madness. What have they done for the gods to disfavour them like this?'

'You may be right,' concurred the judge.

'Grant them a few days respite. Let the wrath of the gods subside. Let this lunacy run its course.'

'Respite would be futile,' said the judge. 'At this stage, the insanity is always fatal. You don't know this lot like I do.'

Maximilian felt his energy drain away. Haunted by Judah's bloodied face, he sat back down.

'This one,' declared the judge, 'he is the worst.' He glared at Judah. 'He is the mother of all these miscreants. Once he is gone, the others will scatter, like rats deserting a sinking ship.'

'Your Honour –' interjected Maximilian feebly.

Ignoring Maximilian, the judge vented more of his wrath on Judah. 'The law decrees that you shall not be punished more severely than your prophet. But don't expect anything less.'

He then turned to Maximilian and acknowledged him. 'I presume you know what happened to their prophet?'

Silently, Maximilian nodded.

'You, propagator!' the judge thundered with finality. 'The death of these citizens is on your hands. In return, you shall perish. The court has passed its verdict. At the glorious festival of Mars – on the twenty-first of March – you will die on the cross.' He slammed his book shut. 'Take them away.'

As he was dragged away, Judah looked almost triumphant.

'Judge Gaius,' said Maximilian, 'I will also take my leave.' As much as he tried to control himself, his voice shook.

'The heretic seems to have affected you,' observed

the judge. He leaned closer to Maximilian. 'Between you and me, he was right on the mark about our gods. I haven't bothered to sacrifice to them in months.' He lowered his voice almost to a whisper. 'Honestly, I don't really believe in them anymore, but better our gods than theirs.'

'However,' he continued vehemently, 'their claims are rubbish. They are superstitions, the same as ours. But while our superstitions bring order to the populace, their superstitions pose a grave danger to the state.' He searched Maximilian's face for some sign of agreement. 'Do you not agree?'

Maximilian knew he was supposed to agree, but nothing could have made him acquiesce at that moment. 'Let's discuss it later,' he urged. 'Right now, I have to go.'

'As you wish,' said the judge. 'You have honoured us with your presence.'

'Until we meet again,' Maximilian replied.

Maximilian could not have extracted himself from the courtroom fast enough. *I can't keep silent anymore*, he thought, the same words burning over and over again in his mind. Yes, Judah was going to die, but at least he would die a free man. He would face God having preached his faith to the world. He would be remembered as a heretic... but not a coward.

He was tired of living a double life, of swallowing insults to his faith, of watching his close friends die. He wanted to scream his identity to the world, to be free, to throw the garb of secrecy into the face of the Roman tyrants. Let them stone him, crucify him if they wished. Unlike them, he had hope in his afterlife.

Suddenly, a thought came to his heart, as if from outside. *What does God want from you?* He knew what he wanted. But what did God want?

He knew the answer. As much as he wanted to run away from it, a small but certain voice spoke to him from deep inside his heart. *You must wait.*

VI

THE GAMES

O n the twenty-first of March, Iamelichos returned to Philadelphia. The Festival of Mars was in full swing. Even from afar, the shrieks of flutes and the rattle of tambourines assailed his ears. As decreed, a glistening new statue of Janus peered down at him from the city gates. It was a far cry from the asceticism of the cave.

Atypically, an elite guard was patrolling the guardhouse. 'Hail, mate!' the commander called.

'Hail,' replied Iamelichos wearily, dismounting his horse and handing over the reins before making the requisite trudge up to the Temple of Janus. Janus was so important to the Romans that they had named a month after him, January. The harsh sun glinted off the freshly washed marble, hurting his eyes. Recent imperial decree demanded that all pay their respects to the gods or face arrest on charges of Christianity. Of course, Iamelichos highly doubted that any of these soldiers would dare lay a finger on him, but he was sure that any negligence would soon be noted. The last thing he needed was to be dragged before a temple tribunal to prove his allegiance.

The temple reeked of incense and blood. Drawing aside the heavy burgundy curtains laced with gold brocade, he unceremoniously dropped to his knees and mumbled a few obsequies. Neither one of Janus' unsettling twin faces replied. On his way out, he nodded cursorily to Bertus – who, to no surprise, was presiding over the temple altars – and tried to avoid taking pleasure in Bertus' miffed scowl. Iamelichos had no interest in exchanging the usual pleasantries due to someone in Bertus' position; he had no interest in letting Bertus think he could use Iamelichos' acquaintance to further his ambitions.

'Fear not!' jibed the commander as Iamelichos rushed down the temple steps and vaulted onto his horse. 'The games don't start till noon.' Wincing, Iamelichos thanked him before disappearing into the streets.

Even if he had actually wanted to have been on time, the immense crowds would have prevented it. Hordes of musicians and dancers were parading around, blowing horns and banging drums. Leaping priests leapt with vigour, hoisting iron shields over their heads in commemoration of Mars, the god of war. Noblemen and commoners alike swarmed towards the amphitheatre in anticipation of the gory spectacle. Everywhere, petitioners were taking advantage of this auspicious day to seek blessings from the gods, and the gutters ran red with sacrificial blood.

One such offering struck Iamelichos with particular disgust. As he waited for the devotees to disperse from the Temple of Apollo, several sinewy slaves held down a very large dog on behalf of their master. The dog was fighting and growling, saliva oozing from its mouth. As a seasoned priest held up a rare pewter vessel sanctified with golden engravings of the gods, an acolyte circled him, carefully chanting ritual incantations. After each stanza, the acolyte dipped a ceremonial goblet into the vessel, filled it with pure ruby red wine, and then sprinkled it onto the sacrificial platform. As soon as the acolyte had concluded, the priest ordered the slaves to lay the dog onto the sacrificial platform. The dog renewed its struggle, drawing blood from one of the slaves. Unfazed, the priest wielded a shining dagger and slashed its neck, the blood spurting out the colour of the wine. Howling, the dog twitched violently before falling still. *Poor animal,* thought Iamelichos, as its owner triumphantly lifted his arms to the sky. 'O Apollo, son of Jupiter! O bearer of the sun in your luminous chariot beneath your father's watchful eye! O, mightiest of the gods, at whose spears and whips the other gods tremble. Behold, your promised sacrifice! Guard my interests, and I will gladden you with strong, sharp-toothed dogs and more. I will overwhelm the Temple of Delphi with silver and gold.'

Iamelichos suspected that the slave-owner was seeking the sun-god's aid for a business venture. Such a gruesome appeal to such an impotent deity whom a mere human had fabricated. These gods had eyes that could not see, ears that could not hear, noses that could not smell, mouths that could not eat, tongues that could not talk, hands that could not talk, and legs that could not walk. They were as far from God as the skies were from the Earth. *No one can perceive God in any way,* Jesus had said. *I shudder to describe him.* This much seemed obvious to Iamelichos. So why did others feel the need to fashion gods in their own image? Was it because, deep down, they really worshipped themselves?

This ignorance has spread its roots deep in the human soul, he reflected. *Will the Christians ever be able to replace the rule of falsehood with the rule of truth?* His appeals turned to God. *God, how will you rectify this corruption? I wish you would clear this gloom which hangs heavy in my heart.*

The way parted as the inebriated spectators moved on to a new attraction. As Iamelichos spurred on his horse, a cart wheeled by, bearing the dog's carcass. It was headed towards the crematorium.

Across town, Diocletian had settled himself in the amphitheatre. Decked out in his fineries, he was eating and drinking more exuberantly than usual. The city elite filled the special stalls around him. Hastily, Iamelichos edged in, in a failed attempt to shield his tardiness.

'Busy morning?' Julian whispered. 'You missed the war dance.'

'I saw it in the streets,' muttered Iamelichos, grateful for the barrage of horns that interrupted him as athletes from as far as Anatolia and Britannia flocked onto the fields for the opening ceremonies of the 227th Olympic games. Discuses flew. Carts raced. Hurdlers hurdled, and wrestlers pummelled each other to the ground. It was impressive — but hardly what the audience had gathered for.

As casually as he could, Iamelichos leaned over to Julian and whispered, 'What's the schedule today?'

'Slaves and Christians,' Julian informed him. Iamelichos flinched at the blatant response. 'The slaves were caught escaping town. The Christians were caught at some ritual. A *revolting* ritual, the commander called it. No surprise — when His Excellency wants Christians, he gets Christians.' He fixed his peculiar gaze on Iamelichos. 'I'm sure you've heard why His Excellency is so happy today.'

Iamelichos tried to shake off the nagging feeling of dread that had pegged him all day. 'Why?' he asked.

'Have a look next time you go out the city gates,' suggested Julian cryptically. 'He'll be hanging right there, dangling from his cross.'

'Who?'

'Diocletian's gift to the Emperor.' Satisfied, Julian returned his attention to the games.

It can't be, he comforted himself, desperately examining Maximilian and Joannes. *They're too calm. Nothing could have happened.* Julian's words kept echoing in his head. Unable to restrain himself any longer, he tapped Maximilian urgently on his shoulder. Maximilian turned around, and Iamelichos saw that his brow was furrowed and his forehead was drenched in sweat.

'What happened?' Iamelichos demanded, his voice barely audible.

Maximilian said nothing.

'Who is it?' Iamelichos insisted. 'Who got arrested?' Maximilian still remained silent. 'Was it...?' Unable to say it aloud, he mouthed, 'Judah?'

The look on Maximilian's face confirmed his fears. 'How can you just sit there?' Iamelichos retorted.

'Calm down,' Maximilian ordered, a strange emptiness in his voice. 'We did what we could.' Iamelichos had never heard him sound so helpless.

We did what we could. How often had those words ripped through his heart. So many of their brethren had been lost throughout the years. But Judah – Judah was unique. He was a brother, a guide, a teacher, a leader, a visionary. He lit the way for the blind, made the deaf hear. His fiery words warmed – but also scorched – illuminating all that he met. To Iamelichos, he was also simply a friend.

They had argued incessantly when they had first met – mostly, over Paul. He still remembered the day Judah had conceded, repeating again and again, *God sent Jesus, not Paul.* Thereafter, he never quoted any of Paul's sermons again, saying they were tainted.

Now, he too would be gone – another dying spark, another casualty of the sacred mission. Grimly, Iamelichos wondered whether he would be next.

A metallic clang brought Iamelichos back to the

moment, and he realized that the athletes had been replaced by a gargantuan metal cage. As the horns blew, a slave was thrust out into the arena, and the cage door swung open. Slowly, a lion peered out, surveying this sudden possibility. After one look, the slave bolted, and the lion waited no more. Gracefully, it leapt through the air and dashed its prey to the ground, snapping the slave's neck into an impossible position. Then, it dragged its kill off to its makeshift den to feed in private – perhaps ashamed of what the humans were applauding for.

The next combatant did not flee. As a leaner, hungrier lion pounced on him, he grabbed its belly and threw it aside. The audience roared, delighted at his unexpected valour. Swiftly, the lion regained its footing and stared him in the face, man and beast locking eyes. The lion lunged again, the slave feinting to the left before leaping to the right. He almost escaped – except the lion caught his foot in its mouth and began hurling him around. As the flesh began to tear off his leg, he screamed, and the lion slammed him down, taking a proper mouthful before dragging its conquest back into its cage.

The afternoon sun was beginning to dip as the arena was cleared out for the finale. Drinks of vinegar and wine were circulated. Fresh beasts were wheeled in, and the final victims were led out to the field. Badly wounded, they appeared oblivious to the clamour. Unlike the slaves, their hands were bound. Hoots and jeers greeted them, and some rubbish landed on their heads.

Iamelichos wanted to flee, to escape, to never return to this hell again. But he had to stay. *God*, he implored silently, sitting there paralyzed among the screaming crowds, *when will this ever end?*

He shut his eyes, but he could not shut out the noise. The tired horns tooted their dreadful last, and he heard the familiar metal clang. Screams and roars assaulted his conscience, and all his slaughtered brethren marched one by one before his closed eyes, their tortured faces pleading for the help that he could not provide.

The noise subsided, and he felt a touch on his shoulder. He looked up. Joannes was standing over him, tears welling from his eyes. The games had finished.

VII

THE PARABLE

Judah surveyed his sleeping cellmate from the wall he was shackled to. Although he had no true way of measuring the passage of time, he was certain he had barely slept for days. It wasn't just that he was forced to stand, but every time he drifted off, the iron bit into his already raw wrists. Exhaustion alternated with pain, and he drifted in and out of consciousness.

His cellmate was moaning deleriously. For days, Judah had comforted him with promises of eternal life, but now, he barely had the strength to stand. Still, he could not ignore the wracking cries. 'Isaac!' he voiced weakly. 'Wake up!'

Lifting his head, Isaac gazed up at him forlornly, tears flowing from his eyes. 'Why doesn't God care about us? Why has he forsaken us?'

'He hasn't forsaken us,' Judah promised. 'He has strengthened our faith and promised us his mercy. Soon, he will release us from this wretched place and take us

THE IDOLS WILL FALL

to his loving side. What more could we ask?'

Subdued, Isaac leaned up against the damp wall and wrapped his shivering arms around his torso. 'Speak to me,' he implored.

Judah hesitated, and not only because of the pain. Doubt vied with his desire to speak. Should he really put this on Isaac now? *If not now, then when? As long as I am alive, my mission is not done.* 'Isaac, my clear-sighted brother,' he finally confided. 'I need to explain something to you so you can surrender your soul to God with steadfast faith.'

'Steadfast?' Isaac repeated, looked at Judah as if he had gone insane. 'We aren't steadfast enough?'

'Years ago, my own friends explained this to me,' Judah continued, 'and now I would like to do the same for you.'

'We are about to die,' Isaac objected. 'What use are explanations?'

'Death is always near,' Judah reminded him. 'All those who live will join us soon. Now that you are about to die, you understand this.' Isaac nodded. 'No one lives forever. So you have two hours or two days or two years or two centuries left. Does it matter?'

'No,' conceded Isaac.

'So why should anyone bother doing or knowing anything if they're just going to die?'

'That's different,' said Isaac. 'I don't know how, but it is.'

'I'll tell you how,' pressed Judah. 'The further away death seems, the more they neglect it. Otherwise, they'd all be like you right now.' Despite his condition, Isaac looked mildly embarrassed. 'Jesus said: *I wish each man would die once and then return to live so he would learn how to live.* Now that your life is about to end, you have realized how meaningless everything they say and do is. Only that which carries to eternity has any use.'

'And what you are going to tell me is useful for eternity?'

'Yes.'

Isaac gazed up at Judah expectantly, like a schoolboy waiting for his teacher. 'Well?'

'Well,' Judah hedged, 'it's about... the... the way you believe in Jesus.' Isaac looked perplexed. 'Isaac,' Judah continued, 'where does the Bible ever say that Jesus asked us to worship him?'

'Nowhere,' replied Isaac mutely.

'So how can you be sure Jesus claimed divinity?' Isaac did not answer. 'How can you be sure he nullified Moses' law? Did you ever once hear of Jesus violating the law, eating pork or breaking the Sabbath?'

'But this is what our holy men have taught us. Paul himself has enlightened us about this,' objected Isaac.

'Isaac,' said Judah seriously, 'Do you know why Christianity spread so fast?' His hands shook the shackles. 'Do you?'

Isaac spoke solidly. 'Because it is the truth.'

'Is that why?' Judah admonished. 'Or is it because we have stuffed Christianity full of pagan beliefs? The idolaters found Christianity in keeping with their own beliefs, so they accepted it. But what they accepted no longer resembled the religion of God.'

Settling himself back down on the putrid floor, Isaac chewed over Judah's words. At length, he asked, 'Which ideas came from the pagans?'

'You should know,' rebuked Judah. 'Only the pagans would give God a child. We have brought this heathen belief into our religion.'

'It is true,' admitted Isaac. 'The Romans call Apollo the son of Jupiter.'

'And the Indians call Krishna the son of God. So when you tell them Jesus is the son of God, of course they convert. But what use is their faith? This is their own religion, not the religion of God.' Intense grief flowed through him, as if the waste of Jesus' anguish was contracting his throat. 'Faith is supposed to lead people to God, not to bring God down to the level of people. Religion has come to uplift humanity, not debase it.'

An incessant drip punctuated his words, and it was as if one or two of the condemned might have been listening. Judah began again. 'Isaac! Did Jesus come to repeat the legend of Attis?'

'Absolutely not.'

'But do you know what the legend of Attis says?'

'Of course.' Folding his arms like a schoolboy, Isaac recited, 'Attis is the god who was sent to Earth and was killed. After three days, he was resurrected and ascended to the Heavens.'

'And when was he killed?' Judah demanded.

'Black Friday.'

'And when was he resurrected?'

'Sunday.'

'And when is this celebrated?'

'Every year, at the beginning of spring. But I still don't see what this has to do with Jesus.'

'Mark my words,' swore Judah, 'it won't be long before the Christians take their Sabbath on Sunday and celebrate the Resurrection with the devotees of Attis.'

'That could never happen,' objected Isaac. 'Everyone knows the Festival of Attis is a pagan holiday.'

'How can you be so sure?' asked Judah. 'Look at what else has crept into our faith. The Father, the Son, the Holy Ghost. Who came up with that? The Romans believe in the triad of Jupiter, Juno, and Minerva. The Indians believe in the trinity of Brahma, Shiva, and Vishnu. A coincidence?' He coughed again. 'Look at what we have wrought'

'Judah,' Isaac said in a tone of utmost seriousness, 'these beliefs are what we are about to die for. Are you telling me they are wrong?'

'You are dying for Jesus, not these illusions,' replied Judah. 'Jesus was a guide. He was not God. He was human! O God, how can your creatures see you as one of them? When will they outgrow these childish thoughts?' He paused, waiting for his anger to subside.

Time passed. Muffled footsteps shuffled up and down the corridor. The cold crept further into their bones. But, for the first time since entering the gaol, Isaac forgot his fear. He was in utter shock. He had literally sacrificed his entire life for the message. He had lost his friends, his family, his home. He had been exiled and landed in Philadelphia as a labourer. And yet, he had never complained. Jesus' teachings had brought him warmth throughout the lonely nights. The Romans had never been able to make so much as a crack in his faith. And now… Judah was telling him it was wrong. All those years, could he truly have been wrong?

He knew the answer, just as clearly as he had known the day before this wretched imprisonment. 'Why did you have to tell me this now?' he voiced. 'Couldn't you have let me die in peace?' Judah did not respond. He came close to Judah. Judah's face was peaceful and motionless, and Isaac feared that he had lost him.

No, Judah was still breathing. Isaac hated to disturb him, but he knew they only had moments left. Now that the pebble had been cast off the top of the mountain, the avalanche could not be stopped. 'So what about the Bible?' he asked loudly. 'Are you telling me that's wrong too?'

Judah opened his eyes, wincing. 'What?'

'The Bible,' Isaac insisted. 'Is it wrong too?'

'No… yes… no…' Judah murmured. Slowly, Judah's countenance transformed back into that of the teacher, and Isaac admired his fortitude. 'Have you ever heard of the Gospel of Barnabas?'

'Who hasn't?'

'And have you ever heard that Barnabas had a row with Paul?'

'I have,' Isaac asserted.

'When Paul was a Jew, he used to persecute

Christians,' said Judah.

'I know,' Isaac said.

'After he repented and turned to Christianity, he and Barnabas started spreading the message together.'

'But they got into a big argument,' Isaac interrupted. 'I know all this. Barnabas went with Mark to Cyprus, where he was killed.'

'Correct,' Judah confirmed. 'And, after that, we hear of Barnabas no more – only Paul and Paul's teachings. Tell me, why should two holy men quarrel? At least one of them had to have been wrong. Why should we assume Paul was right when Barnabas heard Jesus' words with his own ears?'

Isaac did not know what to say.

'I am not saying Paul had bad intentions,' Judah admitted, 'but you need more than good intentions to teach faith. Do you know what Barnabas said about Paul?'

'No.'

'Heed what he wrote in his Gospel.' Judah began to quote from memory, word for word.

> Dearly beloved ... many, deceived by Satan, are preaching a most impious doctrine under the guise of piety. They are calling Jesus the son of God, abandoning the circumcision which God has ordained for ever, and permitting unclean meats. Amongst them, I must regretfully include Paul. I do not speak without grief. But I am writing the truth which I have seen and heard from Jesus so that you may be saved, so that Satan will not deceive you and you will not perish under God's

retribution. Beware those who preach new doctrines contrary to what I write, so that you may be saved eternally. God be with you and protect you from Satan and every mischief. Amen.

The prison was silent, as if the walls were hanging on to every word. 'Barnabas really wrote that?' asked Isaac.

'At the very beginning of his Gospel,' confirmed Judah. 'And do you know what he meant by *new teachings*?' Pain silenced him again.

'Judah,' repeated Isaac, 'we are about to die for upholding these beliefs. How can I face the crucifix knowing that everything I held was wrong?' His words rushed out before he could stop them. 'Am I still a Christian?'

He thought Judah would chastise him again, but he did not. 'Isaac,' Judah replied simply, 'when a building falls into ruin, you must build it anew. There is still time. Faith is a gift of God. It does not come from men. Do you still believe in God?'

'Certainly.'

'And do you believe that he chose Jesus to bear the message?'

'Without a doubt.'

'And do you believe that only through following Jesus can we attain bliss?'

'Yes.'

'So all I am saying is that we have to understand Jesus' message properly.'

Isaac's reflections felt like defeated, scattered troops vanquished by Judah's assault. 'Your words cannot be wrong,' he replied in a tone clouded and cold. 'I just need some time to think. Unfortunately, time is what we do not have.' He tried to think, but all he could think of was how little time they had left. 'Of course, we are facing the crucifix for Jesus. And, up there, we will have as much time to think as we could ever want.'

Just then, the sound of a key smothered his words. As Isaac's heart pounded, the rickety door swung open and five guards entered. Silently, one unshackled Judah. Judah slumped over in relief. Two others threw a rope around his neck, and two more bound Isaac's hands. Then, they were led from the gloom and the filth into a military carriage waiting at the prison gates.

No one spoke as they headed north to the outskirts of Philadelphia, just outside the city gates. Now and then, Judah tried to solace Isaac with a kind glance or a smile, but Isaac's desolate and wearied expression did not lift. Worn crosses rested at the side of the road, discarded after serving their purpose. Then, the carriage halted. Three freshly hewn crosses stood at attention in front of them.

As the soldiers removed the ropes, Judah's face radiated tranquillity, and even hope. 'We are about to meet God,' he murmured to Isaac, 'and behold his beloved visage.'

The soldiers ignored him. Out here in the desert, heretics could say whatever they wanted. Isaac, however, did not seem to hear. He did not even seem to notice as he was lifted to his death. But as the soldier methodically pounded the first nail through his flesh, an agonizing moan escaped from the depths of his being. Ruthlessly, the soldier forced the second nail into his bones, and, mercifully, he passed out.

Alone now, Judah faced the soldiers with no fear. As he was borne to his cross, he thought only of Jesus. Then, for the first time since his arrest, he truly slept. The pain, the exhaustion, the responsibility, the hunger – all of it had conspired to cloud his senses, and his soul rejoiced in its newfound freedom, taking flight from the confines of his physical self.

But a sharp prickling was forcing him back to this world. As much as he yearned to ignore it, it stung his face and bones.

Slowly, the cool morning breeze wafted into the sphere of his corporeal self. Alas, its caress could not soothe his wounds. His limbs were numb, and he could not lift his head. Somehow, it did not seem to matter. The prickling intensified, spiking into sharp shoots of pain. Then he saw a stone whizzing through the air towards him, and he understood.

His head hanging heavily down, he could barely make out a soldier arguing with a group of Jews at the foot of his cross. Not just Jews, but Pharisees – the most orthodox high priests. Slowly, their monotonous buzz shaped into words.

'. . . He's already half-dead,' the soldier was insisting.

'Then what's the problem?' the Pharisee argued. As his vision sharpened, Judah saw that all the Pharisees were clasping stones. 'This damned fellow has led our people astray. We demand retribution.'

'This is Rome, not Judea,' countered the soldier — whether out of pity or duty, Judah could not tell. 'He has been punished under Roman law, and you have no right exceed it.'

You are arguing over the deceased, Judah tried to admonish them, but no sound came out. Silenced, he tried again, hearing only a vague whisper. The quarrel continued, unabated. Finally, he forced all his remaining strength into sound and uttered, 'Let.. them... throw... stones.'

The Pharisee looked up, and then the soldier, and then the entire crowd, their faces registering complete shock, as if a corpse had spoken.

'Let them throw stones,' Judah uttered again. His head would not move, but he still had breath. 'Let them humiliate me now. They shall soon be humiliated in the court of God.'

'He thinks he can tell us about God!' exclaimed the Pharisee to the astonished onlookers.

Judah gasped for air. 'God has no need of your superficial worship. You think you are pious, but you have lost your own souls. You obey the law but have forgotten God.'

A murmur went through the crowd.

'So today you throw stones!' Judah's voice descended for all to hear. 'Yesterday, you tried to crucify your prophet Jesus who came to breathe life into the dead rites of your religion. You are dead, all of you. You are walking dead, so you like death. Die like me, if you really have faith. But you are scared to let go of your souls, so you cling to this semblance of religion. Deceive yourselves, if you wish, but you cannot deceive God.'

A stone slammed Judah in the forehead. 'Shut up!' the Pharisee yelled. The soldier's hand strayed to his hilt.

'You call yourself a Pharisee?' Judah answered back, heedless. 'Do you even know what a Pharisee is?' They all stared up at him. 'A Pharisee is the one who seeks only God and forsakes all for his love. All holy men were Pharisees. They were nothing like you. Tell me, what does your heart desire?'

'I'm going to kill him,' swore the Pharisee.

'Let him go,' the soldier ordered. 'I told you, he's about to die. Leave him.'

The others were silent, listening even. 'Our Lord Jesus has taught us how the true Pharisees live:

They arise from the table still hungry. Each day, they are mindful that they may never reach the morrow. When night comes, they make the ground their bed. Sleeping on a pile of dust behoves a pile of dust. Two hours of sleep should suffice. They have no enemy but their own souls. They accuse none but their own selves. They tremble when they stand to pray as if they were standing on Resurrection Day. Thus, act according to the laws God presented through the hands of Moses, and you shall find God.

So now, let me ask you, are you truly Pharisees? One or two of you, maybe. One or two in a thousand. The true Pharisees have become so rare that you cannot recognize them anymore, but their light shall shine brightly in heaven.'

'You illiterate infidel!' shouted another man from the crowd. 'Who are you to tell us who we are?'

'Behold, the legacy of Jesus of Nazareth,' the stone-thrower decreed. 'Jesus gave these plebeians the audacity to speak against our scribes and our jurisprudents – and our Pharisees.'

'Curse Jesus!' called another.

'That's enough, now,' the soldier intervened, beckoning to a guard across the way.

The dispute was so heated that none noticed a young Pharisee standing alone, staring unblinkingly up at Judah. His wet cheeks bore witness to the turmoil that Judah's words had stirred in the sea of his soul, as if the turbulent waves were splashing forth from his eyes. Judah's words had carved themselves onto the unwritten plaque of his heart.

'Let's go,' shouted one of them, as reinforcements arrived. 'This fellow wants to talk nonsense into the night.'

A preacher to the end, Judah called after him, 'Wait! I will tell you a proverb.'

'The gentleman on the cross has idle time,' one of the youths mocked him. 'Sorry, we're busy, teacher!'

Several of them guffawed. But before they could take another step, the young Pharisee shouted, 'What's your story, Christian?'

'A farmer sowed some seeds. Some scattered and were eaten by birds. Some landed on rocky patches and sprouted, but when the sun shone, the seedlings fell apart, for they had no roots. Some fell between the brambles but smothered as the brambles grew. And some fell on fine earth and germinated: thirty-fold and sixty-fold and hundred-fold.'

'He's a farmer now?' laughed one of them nervously.

'That seed is the word of God, and his farmer is his prophet, my Lord Jesus, who taught:

Whenever you hear the word of God but do not understand it, Satan steals what has been sowed in your heart, and that is the seed that has been scattered and eaten.

Whenever you rejoice at hearing heavenly words, but those words do not take root, those words become the seedlings sprouted up from between the rocks. Their roots have no durability, and they shall perish.

Whenever you hear and believe in the words of God, but the allure of wealth, vanity, power, and worldly desires renders those words useless, those words become the seeds smothered by the brambles.

But whenever you hear the word of God, understand it, and keep it in your heart – that is the seed sown in good earth, and you shall enjoy its fruits.

God has honoured you with his words. He has favoured you with the Torah and his divine teachings. So heed what kind of field your heart will be. Take care that his seeds do not fall into the brambles of your hearts – for that is what has happened to the Pharisees.'

Stones began to fly, the volleys punctuated by Aramaic curses, and a scuffle broke out between the stone-throwers and the Romans. Too late, the soldier returned to duty; he had been gazing up at Judah with a mixture of incomprehension and awe. The young Pharisee too had been busy testing his heart, trying to figure out which field God had sown his seeds in. Blood flowed from Judah's injured body and mixed with the dust down below.

'I read, but you did not listen,' quoted the young Pharisee softly to the youth standing next to him. 'All day, I opened my arms to a group that opposed me rather than embraced me. Now I understand.'

Quickly, the Romans prevailed. But Judah's entire body was covered in blood. Still, hoarsely, he spoke again, his voice so low that it could barely be heard. 'My Lord Jesus has warned: *No one on earth is viler than he who attires himself in scholastic robes to cover his wickedness.*' Then, Judah fell silent, his eyes closed.

When he opened his eyes again, he could not see the mob anymore. But he could still hear them. Suddenly, he realized — they must be harassing Isaac. Rage flooded through him. He commanded his voice to yell, and it partially responded. '*Woe to you, you deceitful scribes and Pharisees who give tithe on cumin and mint but have forsaken justice and mercy!*' Jesus' words flowed through him, strengthening his voice. '*Woe to you who disregard others' rights without a moment's thought! Woe to you who cleanse the outsides of bowls while the insides are brimming with tyranny.*'

Could they hear him? The thought of them hurting Isaac pushed him even harder. 'Woe to you, scribes and Pharisees, whose outsides are as beautiful as tombs, but whose insides are filled with the bones of the dead. Woe to you who frequent the prophets' graves and adorn the tombs of the pious. You swear that, had you lived among your forefathers, you would have never shed the prophets' blood. You confess that your fathers murdered the prophets. You vipers born from serpents! How will you escape the torment of hell? Woe unto you...'

His voice faded to a whisper. Finally, his lips stopped moving. His head hanging heavily from his frail neck, his soul again wandered.

VIII

THE GARDENS

Three days had passed since the gory festival. The morning star was still shining above the crimson dawn when the imperial convoy trotted out its pomp and glory en route to the gardens of Abu Nawas. The talk of the town, Abu Nawas had commissioned ingenious greenhouses of real imported Egyptian glass wherein he nurtured water lilies and birds of paradise and other delights foreign to that arid land. Atop his hills, his meticulously tended orchards blossomed well out of reach of commoners and provided all the figs and pomegranates the palace could ever desire. A rare native to hold the governor's ear, Abu Nawas had graciously invited Diocletian for a day's respite a month ago, and Diocletian had finally responded.

Elite sentinels headed the procession, followed by Diocletian. He was reclining atop a silver carriage borne by four sturdy slaves, muscles rippling down their sun-darkened limbs. Trained as beasts of burden, they kept pace with the horses, although they were treated as far inferior – despite the prestige they brought their owners. A similar litter ferried Diocletian's coquettish wife, swathed in a shimmering wrap, her emerald bracelets glistening in the morning light. Next rode the royal entourage – some relaxing in carriages, others poised on exquisite Arabian steeds. Behind them, more slaves carried the women on delicate palanquins, lest the dust spoil the ladies' special fineries. Ceremonial cavalry brought up the rear. But although Abu Nawas' estates were only a couple hours away, Diocletian was taking no chances; an armed guard flanked them on both sides.

Eschewing the luxurious carriages, Julian, Maximilian, and Joannes rode three abreast. A healthy distance behind them rode the inseparable three – Martinos, Exakoustodianos, and Dionysios. Listlessly tailing them was Iamelichos, trapped between two *flamenes* – one, a priest desecrated to Jupiter and, the other, a priest desecrated to Mars; he wasn't sure which one he liked least. Meanwhile, Bertus was pontificating animatedly from atop a bronze litter.

Given the early hour, no one yet had found much to say – save those who habitually babbled much and thought less. A few miles north, however, an inescapable conversation piece reared its head at the side of the road.

'Halt!' commanded Diocletian's spokesman. Slowly, the caravan ground to a standstill. Impeccably groomed faces began peeking out of the chariots to investigate the cause of the delay. Some felt excited; others, saddened;

but almost all felt proud, for there, only a stone's throw away, hung the notorious Christian rabble-rouser, stretched several feet up on a rude cross.

Only Judah's hair fluttered now in the breeze. None could detect his chest's faint rise and fall. Even the flies, the most skilful torturers, seemed to have lost the ability to torment him anymore, for he had slipped into the door of death, and, this time, there was no turning back.

No one could stop staring. From the safety of his carriage, hatred and vanity poured from Diocletian's gaze. 'Pity the poor wood!' he quipped. Strangely, no one responded; it was as if the entire cavalcade had absented themselves. With a flick of his wrist, he commanded the slaves forward. But as the travellers moved on, their eyes strayed back, causing their heads to turn – except for those whose vanity overrode their curiosity.

Iamelichos felt as if he was about to explode. How was he supposed to feign indifference? How could he not breathe a word? Worse, how was he still supposed to pay his respects to these loathsome murderers? *O God, how long must I remain silent?* he pleaded. *How long will my hands be tied?*

Yet a call inside his soul reminded him, *Be patient, Iamelichos.*

Fortunately, no one was paying much heed to him; otherwise, an onlooker would have thought the crucified was his own brother. Discreetly, he drifted away from his rank. Wrapping his kerchief around his nose and mouth like one of the natives – ostensibly, to avoid the stench, but, really, to avoid being known – he cantered back to the cross. Startled, the guard jumped up and hastily saluted. He had not expected this pathetic sight to attract any of the courtiers. Wordlessly, Iamelichos placed a single gold coin into the guard's dirt-encrusted hand. As the young guard bowed profusely, his thoughts on how he would spend the gold shielded Iamelichos better than any mask.

Grimly, Iamelichos approached the cross. Although the wood was still fresh, it had been splintered in several places. Rocks and stones rested at its foot. Blood and dust had painted Judah's countenance a strange hue in the early morning light. Even though his eyes were closed, he did not appear to be at rest. Although a trickle of blood from his left thigh to his foot had dried, insects were still hovering around the sore, pecking out their last meal. Unexpectedly, a drop of blood fell to the ground, and Iamelichos escorted it to the dust with his own tears.

Truly, what could he have done? Iamelichos was only one of a few who sought reform. On one side, the violent masses opposed them; and, on the other, the powerful elite, who would fight for their hegemony until the end. What could anyone do? *Nothing but what we are doing*, he reminded himself sombrely. Judah may have been just another victim, but the sight of him had brought the pain of the entire empire down onto Iamelichos' shoulders.

'Excellency, in a few hours, he'll be gone.' The soldier's voice invaded his privacy. 'They slashed his vein today. Who'd have believed such a frail person could be so tough? His friend over there died last night. They didn't have to cut his vein.'

Iamelichos' formidable stare silenced the guard. Lifting his head towards the sky, he beheld Judah's pained face. 'The earth was not worthy of accepting your demise,' he murmured, 'so the heavens embraced you. A wonder how haughty you stand, Judah! Your loftiness has borne you in life and death. I swear to God, you were one of his miracles. O God, bestow your infinite mercy upon Judah.'

Then, abruptly, he galloped back to the convoy and made no mention of his absence.

Meanwhile, the inseparable three – Martinos, Exakoustodianos, and Dionysios – had slipped into a dangerous discussion.

'Why wait?' insisted Martinos, bursting with youthful exuberance. 'We need to draw our swords against these tyrants now, shed their blood before they shed any more of ours.'

'We will only injure ourselves by untimely unsheathing our swords,' Exakoustodianos reminded him. 'Suppose we kill thirty of them, what then? We can't afford to be emotional.'

'But it's not only us three,' persisted Martinos. 'Philadelphia is full of believers.' He lowered his voice even more. 'I sense that we have brethren in the palace.'

'It is true,' added Dionysios. 'I have been following Iamelichos and his friends for quite a while. Their faces shine with the light of faith.'

'Careful!' admonished Exakoustodianos. 'You will either endanger them – if they really are Christians – or else you will endanger us.'

'Still,' insisted Martinos, 'we can mobilise a larger group – and not just the faithful. The poor and the oppressed will support us.'

'This religious has no roots yet,' Exakoustodianos rebuked him. 'You could rise up for the masses under any banner – except Christianity. And what's the use? As long as this ignorance exists, this tyranny will persist; and the only way to uproot this ignorance is to rise up in the name of Christ.'

'No, we will draw our swords in the name of Jesus,' Martinos swore passionately, planting his hand firmly on his sword-hilt.

'Then those same suffering masses will turn against you,' Exakoustodianos warned him. 'You underestimate their fanaticism. They are just as steadfast in their ignorance as these tyrants are in their tyranny. They would jump at the chance to serve to their deities so they could improve their lot. What better opportunity than to combat us? With their help, Diocletian doesn't even need his army.' He shook his head bitterly. 'Do you really expect these people who stone Christians to follow you?'

'We have to teach them the truth,' Dionysios interjected. 'Make them follow us. These people are not bad; they have just been badly educated. Once they see the truth, they will follow it.'

'Agreed,' conceded Exakoustodianos. 'But this needs

to happen before we draw our swords, not afterwards. Once we raise the sword, we lose the opportunity to talk. If you – '

Exakoustodianos cut his sentence short. A rider passed them by, and he resumed his speech. 'If you want to teach them the truth, you need to do it now, before they kill you too. But you have a big task ahead of you. These people have been brainwashed into thinking that Christians murder, fornicate, and drink at their secret prayer ceremonies.'

'Drink wine and blood at their secret *revolting* prayer ceremonies,' recalled Dionysios.

They rode on in silence, punctuated by the rise and fall of their horses' hooves. Finally, Martinos ventured, 'But I can no longer endure it.'

'Nor can I,' added Martinos.

Exakoustodianos sighed. 'It's not any easier for me,' he admitted. 'I have also wearied of these people. Pray that God shows us a way.' His eyes strayed towards the heavens. 'O God, how will you keep your promise? Would that I knew.'

As the entourage alighted at the estate's elaborate villa, Abu Nawas personally strode out to greet Diocletian. Each of the other guests received a male or female attendant. As they were led to special chambers to freshen up, the palanquins were arranged in orderly rows, and the horses taken to the stables. In all the bustle, only the slaves with the dubious honour of carrying the palanquins were left standing at the gates.

Their muscles were trembling from exhaustion, and sweat had drenched their brows.

'Why are you standing here?' Exakoustodianos finally demanded, sickened at the oversight.

'Excellency, we are waiting,' the slave replied, still trying to catch his breath. Hope filled his eyes. 'Have we your permission to sit?'

'Certainly,' Exakoustodianos replied immediately, his heart shaken by this weary request.

As the slaves gratefully sank onto the dirt, he glanced around to find someone who could give instructions about them. But everyone was busy running around worrying about how to entertain Diocletian.

Suddenly, one of Abu Nawas' slaves hurried towards him. 'Any orders, Excellency?' he asked, fearing a lapse. 'The house is that way.'

Exakoustodianos indicated the slaves. 'Could you look after them?' he requested, without any of the harshness, austerity, or abusiveness generally directed towards the slaves.

'Yes, Excellency,' replied the slave, his surprised expression reflecting genuine respect.

'Good. I am glad to hear it.' The matter settled, Exakoustodianos disappeared into the villa.

Abu Nawas had arranged for a true Roman-style luncheon with a twist. As the guests reclined around the table on velvet couches, slaves brought out course after course ranging from the familiar Roman favourites to the local Philadelphian cuisine while a minstrel chanted epic poetry and a magician juggled whirls of fire.

Hitherto, Exakoustodianos had felt that the worst he would have to fear at these dinner parties was the fermented fish sauce, popular these days among the elite. But then, the slaves produced silver tray after silver tray of a native Philadelphian delight – sheep's brains. His stomach turned, and not only from guilt over the excesses.

At long last, the last orchard fruits were removed, and the guests were allowed a short rest before the gardens were opened. Two hours of sitting and watching Abu Nawas' varied entertainment – however interesting – had utterly wearied them, and, after their heavy meal, a short turn in the garden seemed like an appealing prospect.

In the secrecy of lilies and roses, Dionysios, Martinos, and Exakoustodianos resumed their intimate discussion. Squeezing the utmost benefit from his costly feast, Abu Nawas walked and talked nonsense with Diocletian. Energized, Maximilian, Joannes, and a few others got into a heated debate about whether Spartacus had been a hero or a criminal to lead his historic slave rebellion. Meanwhile, the priests flocked around Bertus – in theory, to absorb his teachings, but, in practice, to increase the likelihood of promotions.

Julian, however, had intentionally chosen Iamelichos' company. Although generally alert to the game of palace politics, Iamelichos had barely noticed. All he could see was Judah's disfigured face.

'Smell this rose, Excellency,' invited Julian, inhaling the scent of a scarlet rose. 'I have never seen the like of this before.'

'Nor have I,' mumbled Iamelichos absently.

'Charming, is it not?' prompted Julian.

'Yes, charming,' repeated Iamelichos. 'I wonder whose blood has flowed through its petals to lend it such a fragrance.'

'Such poetic words,' observed Julian. 'I've never heard a courtier speak like that. You sound more like Judah.'

Judah's name was like a knife ripping through Iamelichos' heart. 'How would you know,' he riposted darkly, 'unless you had sat and listened to his teachings yourself?'

Julian smirked. 'Not me. I do not believe in any religion – and certainly not Judah's. However' – he fixed his scrutinizing gaze on Iamelichos – 'the faithful should watch their words.'

'What do you mean?' Iamelichos asked cautiously.

'Nothing,' replied Julian. 'Palace Christians just need to be a little more careful than plebeian Christians.'

'How so?'

'Palace Christians shouldn't linger in front of crucified heretics.'

Did Julian know? He couldn't have seen him all the way in the back of the caravan. Had he heard something? Was he bluffing?

Iamelichos decided on rebuking him. 'You are embarking on a dangerous farce.'

'My farce or yours?' replied Julian. 'I never joke. For months, I have kept you and your friends under strict observation.'

A flash of learned terror swept through Iamelichos. Instinctively, he looked around for a way to flee, but the jasmine and honeysuckle trapped him.

'Do not be alarmed,' Julian continued. 'I could have divulged your secret long ago. But you know me. You know that I am not in the habit of telling tales.'

It was half true; Julian always loved telling half a tale and leaving his listeners bewildered.

'Besides,' added Julian conspiratorially, 'although you have preferred others over me, we are still friends. I do not intend to set you up on the cross.'

If only he had taken greater pains to endear himself to Julian, or to conceal his faith. He suddenly remembered their conversation in the amphitheatre that fateful day. Now, it was too late.

'Anyway, you are perfectly safe,' Julian asserted. 'No one would believe me if I reported you... as long as you preach about their gods and turn in a few Christians. Are you capable of that, Excellency Iamelichos?'

'You said we are friends,' Iamelichos appealed weakly. 'Why such venom?

'What venom? You know how I feel about their superstitions. I do not believe in any god – neither the god of Jesus, nor the god of Homer.'

'And you know what you are accusing me of,' replied Iamelichos, defeated. 'Atheism is not a crime, but Christianity is. Half the palace rejects the Roman divinities. Half the rich and famous follow Epicurus and Pythagoras.' Julian blinked. 'As long as you're not starting a new church, you're free to believe what you like. But not Christians. Do I need to explain more?'

Julian stared into Iamelichos' terrified, angered, saddened eyes. 'Excellency Iamelichos!' he asked. 'Have I really branded you? Are you not a Christian?'

The absurdity of the question struck Iamelichos. Of course, he could continue pretending he was not a Christian, and Julian could never prove anything. Julian would probably never say anything either; he enjoyed his secrets too much. But, then again, Julian was ripe for the message. He had already rejected the pagan beliefs, and Iamelichos had been waiting for the right time to approach him. What better time than now – especially since Julian had started the conversation himself?

Deftly, he made his move. 'So what if I were a Christian?' he conceded. 'What's wrong with that?'

Stunned, Julian just stood there and stared. He never had expected Iamelichos to capitulate so quickly.

'Were I a Christian,' continued Iamelichos, 'we would agree about many things – denying their superstitious divinities, for one. And logic. We would agree that we need to prove our faith with logic.'

'Logic?' repeated Julian, still in shock. 'What does logic have to do with faith?'

'Everything,' Iamblichus assured him. 'Why don't we believe in their gods? Because we can't prove them. Why can't we prove them? Because they aren't real. They're just figments of the imagination. People have invented these illusions and made them their gods. But these illusions cannot guide mankind anywhere. They only exist as long as people believe in them. As soon as they forget them, they are gone. Don't you agree?'

'Partially,' Julian responded. 'I accept reason, and I reject stories. But your god is just another story. The only difference is that you don't build statues of him, because he's invisible.'

'And what's the difference between you and the pagans? Your beliefs aren't any less of a conjecture. Can you prove logically that the world has no creator – especially when logic dictates that a creator must be beyond the world's bounds?'

'If you are right, then logic is useless.'

'This is where your mistake lies,' Iamelichos informed him. 'Your beliefs are not based on logic. You just think they are. Your beliefs are really the product of your own mind, just like the pagans'.'

Julian thought about that.

'As soon as we open our eyes to this world,' continued Iamelichos, 'we perceive the harmony of creation and realize there must be some form of intelligence. People have always believed in God.'

'I have no interest in our ancestors,' interrupted Julian. 'I do not believe in a creator or a controller, and I'm not going to concern myself with futile guesses about how the world was created. Science and learning – these are my guiding lights.'

'But science only discovers. It cannot create or regulate. It can explain the order of the cosmos, but it cannot explain why it is ordered.'

'Maybe it's all just a coincidence,' suggested Julian.

'Coincidence?' Iamelichos rebuked him. 'Didn't you

just say you wanted to follow reason? One coincidence might be reasonable. But the entire universe? Everywhere you look, you see intelligence, efficiency, order, and coordination. How could all that happen without any underlying intellect?'

'No one is denying intelligence,' Julian responded. 'But it's just a part of nature.'

'Then whose handiwork is it? Nature's? Is nature intelligent?'

Sensing he was trapped, Julian did not reply.

'If you say yes, you're just another druid nature-worshipper, and we're just arguing over who God is, not whether he exists. And if you say no, then you are denying the obvious. The cosmic order screams out signs of a greater intelligence. Nature itself, devoid of intellect, could not have produced such order. God has shown us his creations so we can understand him, but the ignorant see only the creations and have neglected the creator.'

'That's not what I'm saying,' argued Julian. 'Nature does not act in vain. It leads everything to perfection.'

'And who has taught nature how to perfect itself? None of your intellectuals can answer that, and we come back to God.'

'But if this god really exists, why do we not see or hear him?'

'You need the right senses to perceive things. You cannot see sounds or hear sights. You cannot feel love with your eyes and ears. Our five senses only allow us to see, hear, touch, taste, or smell material objects. God is not an object. To perceive him, you need another sense.'

'So why bother worshipping something we can never sense?'

'Did I say we cannot perceive him? We can, but in our hearts. As much as you hate to admit it, our intellects are imperfect. But our hearts see differently. Numerous people have sworn that they have perceived and understood him. How do you know they are lying?'

'They have never told this to me.'

Ever so slightly, a slight shyness came into Iamelichos' voice, as if he were revealing a great secret. 'If I told you right now that I have seen God with my entire being, and he is more luminous than the sun, how could you deny it? And why? Does a blind man have the right to deny colours just because he can't see them – especially when everyone else tells him these colours exist?'

Julian pondered this. 'So why be so emphatic about worshipping? Whoever wants to worship can worship. Live and let live.'

'God would certainly leave us to live as we please – if he did not want us to reach perfection. We reach perfection only through understanding and worshipping him. He has bound us humble creatures to His presence, to perfection. What better gift could he give?' Iamelichos' voice turned very serious. 'But we still have to choose. Choosing is part of attaining perfection. You are still free to enter Hell, as he has warned, for Hell is nothing but being distant from his perfection. You will realize this someday.'

'Excellencies!' a servant interrupted, hoisting an ornate mound of home-grown pistachios and walnuts and almonds. They had been so absorbed in their discussion that neither had noticed the lengthening shadows of late afternoon. The servant was probably trying to prod them out of the garden. 'Abu Nawas has prepared a sampling of his signature juices and wines. This way, please.'

'We can talk more about this later,' Iamelichos promised, as, dutifully, they traipsed towards the villa, the servant following behind.

'Of course,' agreed Julian, but with an uncharacteristic lack of assuredness. His beliefs had taken a severe jolt. He didn't want to drink Abu Nawas' wines. All he wanted to do was sit in the garden and think so he could repair the gaps in his beliefs.

From the warmth of the villa, he looked out upon the rows upon rows of flowers and orchards, each perfect specimen lined up impeccably. Before him, a servant proffered a dazzling array of coloured beverages, each presented in a perfectly round cup. *Coincidence?* he thought. Hastily, he pushed the thought away. He had no desire to worship God, and he could never fathom embracing Iamelichos' faith. Even if he grudgingly had to admit to the possibility of a Creator, he intended to remain firmly indifferent.

IX

THE EMPEROR'S VISIT

A t last, the cramped city was receiving the attention it desperately craved. As a civilian army scrubbed the streets, the less fortunate purged the rubbish from its gutters. Soon, the bright fragrances of jasmine and whitewash wafted through the alleys. As housewives leaned out the mud-brick windows to inhale the fresh air, children scampered through the streets and cried, 'The Emperor is coming! The Emperor is coming!'

Janus' twin new faces gleamed down on wayfarers as they came and went. Nearby, Bertus' minions were frantically readying the Temple of Jupiter, for the Emperor himself was scheduled to give sacrifice. After thoroughly scouring the sacrificial pit, they had adorned the altars with orchids and hyacinths, graciously donated by Abu Nawas. A rather promising priest had illuminated the otherwise dim temple with a breathtaking spectacle of candles and mirrors in a glistening impression of the heavens above. The alcoves resounded with eloquent speech as Bertus and his acolytes fashioned words of welcome for the Emperor and his *augurs*, the clairvoyants who shadowed him throughout the lands. Should any of them catch the Emperor's eye, they might possibly become *augurs* too.

Imperial representatives had already arrived at the palace and were carefully inspecting the Emperor's quarters (the best in the palace, of course). As the final touches went into the ballroom, chefs and scullery maids chopped and sliced in anticipation of the grand supper. Restlessly, Diocletian paced the palace, scrutinizing the smallest details. He even went out to the stables, giving the stable-hand a good surprise. Perhaps, just perhaps, if he impressed Hadrian with his administration of the province, he might get out of this desert backwater and into a real position. Who knew – maybe someday he would even have a shot at the Emperorship.

Taking refuge from the chaos, Iamelichos, Maximilian, and Joannes had shared a simple dinner of bread and farmer's cheese and then secluded themselves in Maximilian's library. Long past midnight, their lamps were still burning.

A rap at the door interrupted their intense discussion. 'Come in!' Maximilian commanded.

The heavy wooden door creaked open, and his antiquated servant Yunes stepped in. 'Sir, if you do not require anything more, I will retire.'

'An hour ago, I told you that you could retire.'

'I thought you might need something.'

'No, nothing. Thank you.'

Maximilian trusted Yunes implicitly. They often worshipped together in the secrecy of their own home. Still, he waited for Yunes to shut the door before continuing. No one could hear what they were discussing that night.

'Look inside yourselves,' Maximilian urged. 'We have to be sure this is the will of God, not just our own will.'

'Our presence at the palace serves no purpose anymore,' Joannes insisted. 'Our silent agreement only feeds their ignorance, cruelty, and stupidity. It is time for us to break our silence.'

'The public looks up to us,' added Iamelichos, 'whether we deserve it or not. This will be a tremendous blow to the pagans. Should we die, our deaths will only strengthen the Christian cause.'

Joannes spoke ardently. 'Hadrian's banquet is the perfect place. His courtiers will have no choice but to accept the truth.'

'Don't be so sure,' Maximilian warned him. 'You need an open mind to be convinced by logic. A thousand miracles cannot sway those who have dedicated themselves to disbelief.'

'We must speak, whether they listen or not,' replied Iamelichos softly. 'We must do the work of the Prophets. Besides… we can't make the situation any worse. If Julian has already guessed our true faith, it is only a matter of time before others do as well. We cannot risk being unmasked when we are voiceless. We must reveal ourselves while we still can.'

'True,' agreed Maximilian.

'I have never bent my back for another human being,' swore Joannes. 'Should this head bow before the Emperor as it does before God, it is better to be off this body.' Maximilian and Iamelichos murmured in agreement. 'The time of secrecy for the sake of God has ended. Tomorrow, we shall invite the Emperor and his elite to the religion of God.'

The lanterns flickered around them as they thought. Finally, Maximilian concluded, 'We must place our trust in God. He will grant us courage. I hope he accepts whatever we do.'

For the first time since the festival, Iamelichos smiled.

Little did they know that they were not the only ones having the same midnight discussion.

Eagerly, the young and old lined the streets and saluted as Diocletian and his retinue rode out to greet the Emperor Hadrian. Soon, they would lay eyes on the half-man half-god who controlled half the known world.

In no time, the Emperor's mounted guard galloped forth, outdoing the Philadelphians' wildest imaginations. In lavish plate armour, they rode forward in perfect ranks, with pristine feathers capping their helms and polished broadswords hanging at their sides. Behind them, to the beat of a drum marched a battalion of legionnaires, brandishing imposing bronze spears and blood red shields. At the call of a horn, they crouched into a terrifying red and bronze arch, and the crowd went wild.

Suddenly, a blinding mass of gold sailed forth upon the muscular shoulders of twelve Egyptian slaves. An awed hush fell, for none of the Philadelphians had ever seen anything like it. The Emperor himself rode inside the golden frame as a canopy of luscious silks fluttered down over him, swathing him in azure and ivory.

And the entire palanquin was engraved. Etched onto the side, Mars vanquished scores of demigods while Apollo drove his sun-chariot across the luckless foes, his golden rays reflecting off the rivers of blood. From the billowing canopy, Jupiter cast down bolts of lightning while Neptune struck his trident onto the velvet, an army of sea horses and starfish surging to his call. All around, Aphrodite's spells of love chased Athena's owls of wisdom in a never-ending pursuit. Those with delicate taste could have peered at the chariot for days, for such work was not to be found in Philadelphia. Only the best Greek artisans could produce such engravings.

The Emperor's wife was borne a lighter golden palanquin, this one draped in coral and silver. Then followed the enviable *augurs*, chanting blessings for good omens. After them, Diocletian and his retinue reappeared. Ignoring the crowd's cheers, Iamelichos and his friends rode on with particular gravity. A bastion of richly clothed attendants and a rank of armed sentinels took up the rear. It was truly a display worthy of the Roman glory.

Despite their best efforts, however, the Philadelphian streets really could not handle such splendour. Even the surprise shower of flowers at the Temple of Mithras fell short when the procession had to break rank to fit into the narrow lanes. Perhaps Philadelphia's founders had been less ambitious than the Romans. Perhaps they had never thought their humble settlement would host a day such as this. Who would have imagined that, one day, Philadelphia would be conquered by the offspring of Romulus – Romulus, who had suckled wolves' milk? Who would have imagined that, one day, their cobblestones would quake under the wheels of carriages engraved with the gods of Homer?

With regal dignity, the Emperor and his wife ascended the palace stairs. Gone were the novice guards; in their place, stately soldiers clad in silver and red curved up the magnificent stairs, sheltered by a human tunnel of swordsmen. It was truly a sight to behold, although the Emperor took no notice. Then, the imperial party disappeared into Diocletian's private hall.

The Emperor's eyes flickered across the ornate columns and mosaic floor. 'Not a bad place, Diocletian,' he pronounced. 'You can't be having that bad a time out here.'

'Thanks to you, Sir,' replied Diocletian, grinning broadly. He had long been one of Hadrian's highest ranking officers. 'I believe his Highness the Emperor may be tired. Your chambers are this way, sir.' As he personally led the Emperor through the immaculate halls, he apologised, 'Please forgive me should the facilities be insufficient. Your Highness must be aware that our amenities cannot be compared to Rome's.'

'It is not important, Diocletian,' Hadrian said. 'It will do for two nights.'

A throng of servants awaited them in the luxurious chambers. Rose petals floated in basins of warm water clasped in their outstretched arms as slave-boys offered washcloths and anointments. Flasks of the finest oils mingled with bottles of Abu Nawas' fresh nectars. A breathtaking rug of fine weave had been unrolled upon the polished floor, and embroidered blankets invited the Emperor to a canopied bed.

'Should your Excellency have any needs,' promised Diocletian, 'our attendants are at your service. With your permission, I will take my leave to prepare for this evening's ceremonies.' His quavering voice betrayed his excitement. 'Your Highness, your devotees will be there to pledge their servitude.'

Nodding in satisfaction, the Emperor took his rest.

Despite the reception, Hadrian was renowned for his humility. He often repeated that he was a man and had to work like any other man. He insisted on walking the streets of Rome on foot (even though his wife did not share the same predilection) and would occasionally exchange greetings with the commoners.

But he would not think of sacrificing his claim to the divinity. Barely a couple centuries ago, the first Roman Emperor had styled himself as Augustus – the sacred – and had named the ninth Roman month after himself.

Augustus' successors had nurtured the tree he had planted, and Hadrian was hardly inclined to cut it. Instead, many of the desperate and ignorant accepted Hadrian into their pantheon as just another god and prayed to him as they did Mars and Mithras.

And who would not enjoy being treated like a god? Only those whom God had looked towards and whose beings were filled with humanity.

As evening arrived, the elite of the elite began trickling into the hall — slowly, so as not to appear too enthusiastic. The great hall dazzled more brilliantly than ever. Silver chandeliers holding a hundred candles apiece illuminated the scarlet red drapes. At the door, servants guided the guests to chairs of silver and gold, studded with garnets and amethysts. Magnificent tables were laid out with saffron sweets and peacock tongues and all manners of exotic delights. At the head of the room, the servants had unveiled a real throne, glowing with the dull, heavy lustre of pure gold.

Feeling like rustics, the aristocracy reminded themselves that it was uncouth to stare. But few could ignore the gold and silver that had been poured into the palace. Dragged from the throats of the Roman conquests, it followed the Emperor from banquet to banquet. Thanks to his visit, that night, they would celebrate the pomp of the world.

Merely being invited would be an honour narrated from father to son. However, Diocletian's hand-picked few would be granted a greater honour: kneeling to the

Emperor to pledge their servitude. Had his chosen elite failed to appear, their heads would have undoubtedly rolled, but few – if any – would have failed to turn up for such a supreme honour.

Envy filled the aristocrats as the Emperor leaned on his throne and bantered idly with Diocletian. Some wished they could be the Emperor himself and have what he owned – or at least part of what he owned. Others just wanted to be on familiar terms with him so he would chat with them like he did with Diocletian. And God only knows what the slaves thought as they served the lavish feast. Perhaps their only hope was to take scraps home to their families.

But, that night, some were nurturing very different thoughts, thoughts that did not belong beneath that roof. Under the Emperor's silk and brocade robes, Maximilian saw a walking corpse. Hidden beneath the earth, it would soon have neither a tongue to protest nor a hand to refuse. Then he foresaw another imbecile seated on the bejewelled throne. And then another corpse and another fool. The departed never warned their usurpers, nor would the latter have heeded their warnings.

All around him, Maximilian saw a people robbed of sense by the glitter of gems and gold. Entranced by a man just like themselves, they had forgotten their Creator who held the entire universe under his control. The costly gems of their souls had surrendered to the Empire's silver and gold.

At another table, Dionysios tapped his fingers

anxiously and downed glass after glass of honeyed nectar to soothe his parched throat. What was he going to do? How could he avoid pledging his servitude? Would they even understand him if he told them that he loathed their stupidity, scorned their power, and disdained their wealth?

O God, he beseeched, why must the servants of truth be weak and destitute while the servants of falsehood enjoy power and prestige? You have promised to make the faithful victorious – but when? And how? How can we crush such a power when we have no power ourselves?

As the royal trumpets blared, Maximilian's heart pounded. Fleetingly, he thought of his wife and child. As if in a dream, he watched Diocletian thank the Emperor for gracing Philadelphia with his presence. Then, the herald proclaimed, 'High Priest Bertus!'

With the dignity particular to priests, Bertus rose from his emerald-studded chair, smoothed his cape, and approached the throne. The audience watched on in suspense. How would he be honoured?

Suddenly, as if on cue, he stopped a few feet before the Emperor. In a motion all Roman aristocrats learned from childhood, he knelt and bowed his head. Then, in a tone of absolute servility, he proclaimed: 'Hail, Divine Emperor Hadrian, the godhead of Rome and the entire world. Hail Jupiter and the deities reigning beneath his exalted might. Hail, ye all, hail.'

His eyes still lowered, he rose and walked backwards several steps before returning to his seat. Excited murmurs ran through the crowd. Who else would be called?

The herald pronounced the next name from his scroll. 'Marcus Julian!'

Julian repeated Bertus' actions to the letter – except that he had a peculiar expression on his face. As he returned to his silver chair, he scrutinized Iamelichos. What was he thinking?

'Abu Nawas!' Apparently, his grand feast had earned him a place on the list. Fastidiously, Abu Nawas mimicked Bertus' obsequies, minimizing his Syriac accent.

And then it happened. *'Maximilianos!'* The three of them looked at each other. Their hearts pounded, and no one moved.

Suddenly, an unexpected serenity settled over them, reassuring them that they had decided correctly. Rising in unison, they approached the throne with solid, fearless steps.

The noblemen gaped. Three, when one had been called? What unique plan had these innovative and clever men contrived for the Emperor's entertainment?

Julian lowered his head.

The Emperor had bent his head to accept their servitude – but in vain. Frantically, Diocletian mouthed to them, 'Kneel! Kneel!' But Maximilian's knowing smile froze him in his chair.

Maximilian's sonorous voice shattered the silence. 'Your Highness!' The Emperor's head snapped up, his face flushed. 'We will never accept any lord but the one

Lord. He has created everything, and we worship none but him.'

Suddenly, Diocletian's eyes widened. 'Gods in Olympia,' someone murmured. Firmly, Maximilian held his ground.

But Diocletian was not staring at him. The whispers grew louder. Hesitantly, Maximilian turned around. There, behind him, stood the inseparable three, like an army dispatched at the last minute for support.

'Your Highness!' Martinos thundered, his voice belying his youth. 'Humans can accept no master but their Creator. A human can never be God. *If horses and cows and lions could draw, they would depict God as one of their own*, Xenophanes said. It is time to rise beyond that.'

'Diocletian,' hissed Hadrian in an undertone, 'what is this circus you are presenting me?'

'They have never acted like this before,' stammered Diocletian. 'Hitherto, they always conducted themselves as your obedient servants.'

Politely, the *Pontifex Maximus* signalled for permission to speak. 'Your Highness, the stupidity of the masses has infected these gentlemen and made off with their sanity.' Hadrian nodded slowly at the high priest's words; perhaps he was right. 'I doubt anyone here denies the Creator of the world. We do not worship stone and metal. The illiterate masses cannot fathom the subtleties of our teachings, so they believe these statues are actually our gods. But our beliefs are much more refined.'

His soothing tones assuaged the Emperor. These six courtiers would soon recognize the error of their ways, and Roman dignity would be restored. 'The Creator has fashioned beings superior to man and placed them in charge of the world. Therefore, we must pray to them, for the Creator has not involved himself in our affairs. Since these great spirits and mighty creatures live beyond our sight, we carve their faces on metal and stone. How else could we adore an invisible god?'

'Present your proof,' Maximilian demanded, and the spell was broken. 'But you will never be able to prove your words, for you are lying. How could God – who is utterly self-sufficient – require aides?'

Before the pontiff could reply, Maximilian gestured towards the Emperor. 'But forget gods of metal and stone. Here, we have a god in the flesh. His Highness has bestowed divinity upon himself. Prove it, then, the same way the prophets proved their claims.'

The Emperor's voice rumbled over him. 'For thousands of years, our forefathers worshipped these gods.'

'Our forefathers were wrong,' Maximilian shot back. 'Why should we err like they did?'

'You ungrateful fool!' Diocletian roared. 'Your honourable fathers walked among the nobility. Have you really converted to the religion of slaves and shoemakers? Alas!'

A servant delicately swabbed Diocletian's forehead with a cool cloth. Roughly, Diocletian pushed him away.

Not deigning to reply, Maximilian forged ahead. 'Does the Creator need his created? How can the Creator be incapable of administering his creation?'

Hastily, the pontiff replied. 'We do not say the Creator lacks power. Rather, he has assigned power to his elite. He is too high to involve himself in the affairs of mere mortals. In exchange for prayers and sacrifices, they bestow upon us power and glory.'

Iamelichos joined the argument. 'How can you prove that? Who has God sent to tell you that he handed the universe over to created beings who eat and sleep and copulate like you do?'

Despite his eloquence, an unmistakeable streak of hatred crept into the pontiff's voice. 'Your great god couldn't even defend his prophet Jesus. Why doesn't he save his own worshippers from the wrath of the servants of Jupiter?'

'Enough!' thundered the Emperor. He turned to Diocletian. 'Why are you sanctioning this? Arrest them immediately!'

A horde of soldiers swarmed towards the defiant six. Swiftly, Maximilian and his allies glanced around. They were unarmed, and they had no possibility of escape. In no time, they were surrounded.

Suddenly, one of the silver clad guards came barrelling in. 'Praise Jesus!' he yelled as he slashed the neck of the first soldier in his path. A sword ripped into his stomach, and he fell to the floor, groaning.

Instinctively, Diocletian's hand grasped his sword as he surveyed the room for further defectors.

A guard wrenched Maximilian's hands behind his back. 'Your Highness!' he called. 'Let me present one last question to the pontiff. Should he answer it, we shall repent and adopt the religion of our forefathers. Otherwise... you must accept the truth of our words.'

'Impudent fools!' muttered the Emperor.

'I beg your pardon,' Maximilian clarified. 'Should his reply be unconvincing, you will leave us free to practice our beliefs.'

'Ask.'

Maximilian looked up at the dais towards the high priest. 'Let me ask you one thing. Did the Creator create these divinities, or no?'

'Yes, he created them, but they are elevated, esteemed, and empowered beings.'

'So if the Creator wills to harm me, can these deities restrain him? Or if the Creator wills to bless me, can they stop him?'

'The Creator himself does not interfere in the affairs of this world.'

'But can God also determine things?'

'Doubtlessly.'

'Then all power rests in his hands, and we pledge servitude only to him. Why should we fear created beings when all of creation bows to the Creator's will?'

The pontiff had no answer. 'Remove these lunatics,' the Emperor demanded.

Silently, the guards dragged them and the victims out. The marble floor was stained with blood. No one dared to speak. Finally, the Emperor commanded,

'Carry on with the entertainment. No one else needs pledge servitude.'

Wine flowed and harpists played – although no one appeared to be listening – as Diocletian swallowed his disappointment. On the night of his triumph, his dreams of power and prestige had shattered into pieces.

X

THE ESCAPE

As soon as the guests had dispersed, Diocletian had hastily retreated to his chambers. Seizing an ornate decanter, he soothed himself in the darkness with unadulterated spirits.

Soon, however, a knock interrupted his daze. 'Your Highness, the Emperor has summoned you.'

Steeling himself, Diocletian followed his servant to the Emperor's chambers. There, the Emperor was waiting with his topmost advisor.

'A wonder to see you, Excellency Diocletian,' the Emperor voiced. 'It's almost as if you were avoiding us.'

'Your Highness.'

'No need for concern. This incident does not involve you. It could have happened at any of our palaces.'

The cooling rain of the Emperor's words soothed the blaze in Diocletian's soul, and, slowly, his ambition began to bud again.

'I have always tried to abstain from making decisions

in two conditions,' the Emperor continued. 'First, when intoxicated, and, second, when furious. Now that my rage has abated somewhat, we must purge our ranks. They are your counsellors, Diocletian. What will you do about them?'

'Whatever Your Highness wishes,' Diocletian replied obediently. 'However, in my opinion, we should make an example of them.'

The Emperor stroked his beard thoughtfully. 'They are noblemen, correct?'

'Yes, your Highness.'

'Then their blood cannot be shed on the quiet. Especially with the imperatorial presence here.'

'Our township is secure,' reassured Diocletian. 'The Christians have no sympathy in Philadelphia.'

'As long as the masses believe they were Christians,' the advisor interjected.

A shadow of concern crossed the Emperor's face. 'Diocletian, be honest here. How much of an outcry would their death cause?'

'Your Highness,' ventured Diocletian, 'in all honesty, I would like to tear them to shreds, limb by limb. But your advisor may be right. They were my most popular counsellors. Iamelichos the virtuous. Maximilian the noble. Joannes the compassionate. Dionysios the thoughtful. Exakoustodianos the upright. And Martinos the youthful.'

There was no mistaking the pain in his voice. 'Some of the soldiers favour them too. News of their arrest must have spread by now. I have ordered my most trusted commanders to be on the alert. If anyone can be trusted after tonight.'

'You are concerned about the Christians?' clarified the Emperor.

'We can handle the Christians,' Diocletian avowed. 'Their numbers are few. They are the poorest of the poor. They can barely afford bread, let alone weapons.'

'Then what exactly is your concern?'

Ever so slightly, Diocletian avoided the Emperor's gaze. 'The ambitious are always a threat.'

'Sedition, you mean.'

Despite himself, Diocletian's anger surged. 'Yesterday, thousands witnessed them prostrate themselves to Jupiter. Today, barely four score saw them sell themselves to Christ. Who is going to believe this farce they pulled tonight?'

'This complicates matters,' said the Emperor slowly.

'But, your Highness,' Diocletian swore, 'we are in a position to handle any incidents. We can and will make an example of these six as a warning to others.'

The Emperor stared Diocletian straight in the eye. 'Then decapitate them immediately.'

'Your Highness!' interjected the advisor. 'Do not make haste. Their antics have fortified the Christian cause and weakened the state religion. Making martyrs out of them will not help.'

'Yes, it will,' swore Hadrian. 'This disease that has plagued the Empire will come to an end.'

'Prudence,' the advisor encouraged him. 'With prudence, we can turn our loss to profit, and their profit to loss. Should they repent publicly, we will emerge victorious.' He paused. 'If they have allies in the army too, that cannot be ignored.'

'And if they refuse to repent?' demanded Hadrian.

'Take them to the brink of death,' proposed the advisor. 'Then, at the last moment, give them hope of life. They will reassess their beliefs. Life is sweet, your Highness, especially for the condemned.'

'Let's hope so,' the Emperor said.

'Even if they refuse to repent,' the advisor continued, 'we will still come out ahead. As soon as they publicly declare themselves heretics, no one will object to their death.'

'But what about the masses?'

'We can keep our hands clean of their blood. Ship them off to Jerusalem, let the Jews take care of them.' He lowered his voice. 'Even if they do repent, we can still get rid of them, one by one, without causing a ripple.'

The Emperor paused, trying to find a flaw in the plan. 'Not a bad idea,' he said tentatively. 'Diocletian?'

'Whatever your Highness commands,' murmured Diocletian.

'For now, you need to take them out of the brig,' the advisor instructed Diocletian.

'Under no circumstances!' objected Diocletian.

'Avoid outcry,' the advisor censured him. 'Put them under house arrest. Tomorrow, let them seek forgiveness from the divinities. If they abdicate Christianity, let them go. Otherwise, let them prepare themselves for a hail of stones.'

'Agreed,' said the Emperor. Reluctantly, Diocletian concurred.

The advisor eyed Diocletian doubtfully. 'And speak to them more. A smooth tongue can soothe a voracious lion.'

The six condemned men stood at Maximilian's threshold as Commander Sanctus ordered a thorough search of the house. A few swords, an axe, and a cleaver were thrown into a pile.

Efficiently, Sanctus had stationed guards at the doors and windows and even on the roof. However, his men treated the prisoners with uncanny deference. None of them actually wanted to stand guard inside.

Despite his fortifications, Sanctus felt uneasy. 'Excellency,' he asked, 'would it be a problem if we stationed a few soldiers inside the halls?'

'Do we have a choice?' Maximilian responded.

Sanctus looked to the floor. 'I am sorry. I have a duty to perform.'

Without saying another word, Maximilian followed his friends inside his home – now a fortified gaol.

Initially, the household had met the guests' arrival with joy laced with surprise. But now, they watched dumbfounded as several soldiers took up guard.

No one uttered a word – except Anna, Maximilian's wife. As soon as the guests were settled, she pulled Maximilian aside. 'In God's name,' she implored quietly, 'what is going on here? What are these soldiers doing in our home?'

All Maximilian said was, 'Bring the guests some refreshments.'

As Anna went off to the kitchen, Maximilian sat with his guests for a couple moments. Then, discreetly, he joined her and told her what had happened.

It would hardly be necessary to explain her feelings. It would not be difficult to guess the emotions of a woman who feared that the coming dawn would lead to the dusk of her husband's life. 'What will you do tomorrow?' she asked chokingly as she struggled to keep waves of tears from falling.

'We will put our trust in God. We have to think long and hard. There may be a way.'

'My God! O, son of Mary! Help me!'

'Fear not,' Maximilian reassured her. 'God's will shall come to pass. Tonight, I felt peace and strength in my heart. I am certain it was from God, and so I am not the slightest bit anxious. Whatever is lost in the path of God does not go to waste.'

'I trust you,' Anna said. 'I know you never act thoughtlessly. I just hope that God will give us patience.'

'God is with us,' promised Maximilian, 'even if the world is against us.'

The tears imprisoned in Anna's eyes streamed down her cheeks.

'Put your hope in God,' Maximilian reassured her again. 'Don't worry. I have a plan.' As Anna's eyes widened in surprise, he followed his aged servant Yunes who was carrying the tray of steaming beverages into the living room.

Fast friends, the two groups of Christians had already acquainted themselves with each other. Neither could believe they had never fully recognized the others before.

Now, Iamelichos addressed them all. 'Friends! The Emperor has sent us here to deliberate, but we have nothing to consider. Tomorrow, we shall meet our Creator and attain our utmost desire. We have nothing to gain by remaining in this world, and nothing to lose by leaving it. Why remain on the path when we can enter into the realm of his worship?'

Martinos could contain himself no more. 'Such good friends God has given us in the last hours of our lives! Let us think of this world no more. When morning comes, we will gladly relinquish it. Ah, what peace I feel tonight! I swear by Jesus, I know not how to thank God.'

'But perhaps God has not ordained death,' interrupted Maximilian, 'no matter how ardently we desire it.'

They all stared. 'What do you mean?' asked Iamelichos.

'If you agree, we will escape.'

'Escape?' Martinos asked in surprise. 'How can we escape? His Excellency has surrounded us with a small army.'

Maximilian lowered his voice to a dead whisper. 'This house has a secret passage.'

A moment ago, they had been ready to surrender

their souls to their true owner. But now, the small chance of life filled them with dread.

Maximilian broke the momentary silence. 'If you agree, I will pack some provisions, and we will be on our way. We have little time left until the morning. We need to take full advantage of the darkness.'

'What about the soldiers?' asked Joannes. 'Where will we go? They will capture us at the first light.'

Again, silenced reigned. The long night that had seemed like it would never end now seemed to be vanishing all too quickly.

Suddenly, Iamelichos spoke up. 'I know of a place. We will go southwards.'

All eyes were set on him. 'About five miles from Philadelphia, there is a village called Raqim. I have a Christian friend there. He will shelter us.'

'We cannot jeopardize other people's lives,' objected Maximilian.

'He is different,' said Iamelichos. 'He will be glad to help.'

'But what about the soldiers?' asked Martinos.

'They will not invade the privacy of our discussions,' promised Maximilian.

Maximilian glanced around at his friends. One by one, he read the agreement on their faces. There was no need to wait. Swiftly, he stepped out and went to his wife who was waiting restlessly in the library.

'We are leaving, Anna,' he said in a whisper.

'Where? How?'

'We will leave Philadelphia tonight. Prepare a little

provision for us as soon as possible.'

'But how will you escape?'

He pointed towards the bookcase. 'We must hurry. Time is short. Make sure you do not arouse the suspicions of the soldiers.'

Quickly, Anna went to the kitchen. Maximilian headed towards the room where his children were blissfully asleep. Softly, he opened the door. Brightening the lamp, he took in their peaceful, innocent faces. It was the look of a father who might never see his children again. Would he ever return? Any return to Philadelphia not twinned with death would require a total inversion of the entire world order. Could it be possible?

Maximilian would have given anything not to leave his children's side. But the thought of God comforted him. Planting affectionate kisses on their cheeks, he turned away swiftly and headed for the kitchen. There, Anna and Yunes had prepared a small parcel of flatbread. Quickly, Maximilian requested Yunes to take the bundle of food to the library without attracting the soldiers' attention.

Then he took his wife's hand. 'Goodbye, Anna. From now on, you are responsible for the children. I know you will take good care of them. Yunes will assist you. As soon as I am settled somewhere, I will contact you.' He did not mention what would happen if they did not escape.

Tears left Anna tongue-tied.

'Be happy,' Maximilian soothed her. 'Whatever

comes from God can only be good. Teach our children to walk and breathe in the path of God. Help them understand that everything is from God. God is more merciful to us than we are to ourselves.'

Still weeping, Anna nodded wordlessly in agreement.

'It's time to go,' said Maximilian, touching her shoulder.

Then, he returned to his guests. 'Let's continue our discussion in the library,' he pronounced. 'Come along whenever you are ready.'

Slowly, the guests trickled towards the library without alerting the soldiers.

Yunes was waiting in the library. With his help, Maximilian slid the bookcase away from the wall. Beneath it lay a dusty trap door, caked with cobwebs. Deftly, Yunes pulled it up by its brass ring, and they stared down into the pitch black cavity.

'Carry on,' Maximilian told them.

As, one by one, they disappeared into the dark underground passage, Maximilian pulled Yunes close to him. 'Signal us when the exit is clear.'

Then, he too dropped himself into the cellar. His small lantern illuminated the mould and spider webs all around them. Their noses tingled with the musty smell of damp earth, and they heard a faint scratching.

All too soon, the passageway came to an end. Uncomfortably, they stood there in the cramped underground space and waited for Yunes' sign. Martinos looked as if he might become ill. Suddenly, the hope-inspiring light of a lantern beckoned them from the other end. Immediately, Maximilian sprang the latch of the trap door above him and pushed. It wouldn't budge. Could there be something on top of it? He pushed again. It still would not move.

God, help me, he implored desperately. His mind began racing. What if they could not get out?

Suddenly, it came free. Hastily, Maximilian put out his lamp, and, one by one, they climbed up a ladder entwined with ivy that pricked their hands as they groped for the rungs.

They emerged into a back alley. The dim starlight outlined a few soldiers standing and chatting, and they immediately scurried the other way. They had to find the quickest way out.

An hour later, the prisoners were still closeted in the library. Suspicious, one of the soldiers peeped into the keyhole. Nothing. Could they really be sleeping at a time like this?

Unable to bring himself to invade their privacy, he instead reported to the commander. Staring at him in disbelief, Commander Sanctus barged into the villa. 'Where is the library?'

'This way, Sir.'

Sanctus pressed his ear to the door. After his knocks echoed back to him, he threw the door open and confirmed his worst fears.

The windows trembled with the roar of his voice. 'Excellency Maximilianos!' He turned to the soldier. 'Search everywhere, Matius!'

'Sir?'

'Search the whole house. The birds have escaped their cage.'

The house burst into chaos. Anna – who had been feigning sleep – rushed instinctively into the children's' room. Tears fell down their cheeks as they stared at their mother with utter incomprehension.

Suddenly, Matius noticed Yunes. 'Move!' he commanded, unsheathing his sword.

Mutely, Yunes hobbled towards the commander.

'Sir,' Matius said breathlessly, 'he knows everything. He was in there with them in the library.'

Santcus glared down at him sharply. 'Do you know the punishment for aiding and abetting the escape of prisoners?'

'Prisoners?' repeated Yunes. 'What prisoners? I haven't been anywhere near the prisons all night.'

'Your master and his friends.'

'My master is in prison, sir?'

Sanctus glowered at him. 'Where is your master?'

'You mean Excellency Maximilianos?'

'Yes.'

'No need to scream,' admonished Yunes. 'He's right over here.'

Sanctus' eyes glittered with the light of hope. Astonished, he and the soldier followed Yunes towards the library.

'I don't understand, sir,' grovelled Yunes. 'He was just here with his friends. Perhaps they are in the living room?'

'Your master has escaped! Are you trying to tell me

you didn't know?'

'Escaped?' echoed Yunes. 'From his own home? I might be a bit dim, sir. Could you speak more clearly?'

'You think you are clever, you stupid old man?' Sanctus growled.

'Sir, this is the home of Excellency Maximilianos, counsellor to his Highness Diocletian. Perhaps I am dreaming. O, heavenly fathers!'

Sanctus ignored him for a couple moments. 'Old man, does this house have a secret passage?'

'All the old houses do,' replied Yunes. 'My God, what is going on here tonight?'

'Take me to it,' Sanctus demanded.

Slowly, Yunes hobbled over to the bookcase. 'It hasn't been used for years.'

Pushing him aside, Sanctus attacked the bookcase. Maximilian's rare collection of scrolls and volumes tumbled to the floor. Clambering over the pile, he lifted the trap door, peered down, and yelled, 'Lantern!'

Matius came running in. Quickly, he grabbed the lantern from the wall and handed it to his commander. Sanctus leaped down. Fresh air assaulted his nostrils as he sped towards the end of the passage, Matius at his tail. Popping open the trap door, he discovered an overgrown back alley.

'Stand alert!' he yelled. The soldiers jumped at his command. 'Search the whole town! Search each of their houses!' He thumped Matius on the shoulder. 'We will capture them tonight.'

XI

THE CAVE REVISITED

Philadelphia soon faded into distant memory as the six fled into the underbrush. As they navigated the dry, uneven lands, brambles tore the fine weave of their delicate cloaks, and they lifted their garments lest they leave telltale threads. Desert larks warbled at their soft footfall, and the occasional rodent skittered out of their path. A sharp breeze blew past them, and the full splendour of the heavens lit the night sky.

Fearing daybreak, Iamelichos sped them faster and faster until, just as the break of dawn, they found themselves in a crackly grain field. It was still dark, and the farmers were still asleep. Quickly, Iamelichos lend them onto a smooth dirt path into the village proper before realizing that, in this dim light, all the mud brick houses looked the same. The smell of fresh bread alarmed his nostrils, and he pressed on, instinctively searching his way. As soon as the village awakened, they would lose the cover of anonymity.

Suddenly, an unimposing square house beckoned to Iamelichos, as if the very streaks of morning light were pointing to it. Praying it was the right one, he rapped on the door. There was no response, and he rapped again.

Footsteps padded towards him, and lantern light filtered through the cracks. 'Who is there?' called a surprised, friendly – and blessedly familiar voice.

'Antonios!' Iamelichos whispered as loud as he dared. 'It's me!'

At the sight of Iamelichos standing there in all his dignity, a broad smile spread across Antonios' lips. 'Excellency Iamelichos! You are most welcome. I was just praying. Come in! Were you at the cave?'

Iamelichos hesitated. 'I am not alone.'

Peering out the door, Antonios nearly fainted. Five imposing strangers in imperial dress towered out of the dust. As he lifted his lantern higher to make sure he was seeing properly, the light glimmered off the golden embroidery of their richly dyed robes. Could he be dreaming?

Hiding his astonishment, he told them, 'Don't just stand there. Come in!'

With full dignity, the strangers filed into his hut and collapsed onto his dirt floor.

'Were you holding congregational prayers at the cave?' asked Antonios. 'I wish you had told me. I would have loved to come!'

Raising their eyebrows, the men turned their faces towards one another interrogatingly.

'Forgive me,' Antonios chastised himself.

However, Iamelichos seemed perfectly at ease. 'We passed the cave in the mountains on the way here. Almost none of the villagers know about it. But you can see the entire village from the cave. I used to take refuge for prayers there, and that was how we met.'

His heart rejoicing, Antonios was dying to ask more, but his sense of good hospitality restrained him. Instead, he contented himself with pouring some water from an earthen jug into an iron kettle dangling over the fire and crumbled some dried mint in. It was all he had to offer.

'With your leave,' he suggested, 'I would prepare some loaves for you to break your fast upon. You have travelled long and far.'

'Antonios,' Iamelichos warned, 'I do not want to mislead you. We have not come as guests. We have come as escapees.'

'Escapees? For what crime?'

'The crime we all share. The Emperor is after our blood.'

'The Emperor!'

'I told these men you might be able to help us.'

'Well, yes, of course,' replied Antonios. 'My home is your home. Excellency Iamelichos, I am honoured to be your servant.'

Puzzled, however, he looked at their lavish, torn, dusty robes. 'Are you all Diocletian's counsellors?'

Maximilian's powerful voice awed him into silence. 'That is not important. But you, Antonios! Do you know the punishment for sheltering fugitives?'

Antonios did not respond.

'You have a future ahead of you,' Iamelichos gently reminded him. 'Do not sacrifice it because of us.' .

'Yes,' Antonios confessed bashfully. 'I soon plan to marry a Christian girl.'

A hint of a smile reached Iamelichos' eyes. 'Good.'

'Still,' declared Antonios – and it was as if all doubt had retreated from his soul – 'you and I are one breath in separate bodies. What is the punishment for giving refuge to one's self? You may stay here as long as you like, even forever.'

'You have truly surpassed the duties of brotherhood,' Maximilian commended him. 'But we cannot stay here. We must move on.'

Just as they had in Maximilian's library only hours before, the six sat and thought. It was as if they had escaped in vain.

A few voices drifted in with the morning light. Blowing out the lamp, Antonios watched with pleasure as the men delicately sipped the steaming tea from wooden bowls. He could not say why he felt such affection towards these unexpected guests. Perhaps because of Iamelichos?

Iamelichos had, after all, left a deep impression on his young soul. He had felt as if he had been searching for Iamelichos his entire life but had never known it. Now, seeing Iamelichos in such peril filled him with such immense sorrow that he would have given the entire world to free Iamelichos from this danger and himself from this distress.

Tracing a small map in the dirt, Maximilian surveyed

their escape routes. 'The Persians lie to the east.'

'They would never welcome us,' Iamelichos predicted. 'Fugitive Roman counsellors – and Christians at that.'

'The Romans hold all the territories to the north,' continued Maximilian. 'We could walk for a year and still be in Roman lands.'

'We could go west, towards the sea,' suggested Martinos.

'With no money?' answered Maximilian. 'How could we buy passage? Our only option is to go south – into Africa, or the Arabian deserts.'

'No,' objected Antonios. 'The deserts are very treacherous. You do not know your way. The nomads would sell you as slaves – if you did not perish from thirst.'

'The African governors would sell us back to Rome too,' added Iamelichos glumly. 'Anything to curry favour with the capital.'

Martinos rubbed his chin. 'We cannot escape without horses and weaponry. Friends! We will be captured... unless God shows us a way.'

As they sat and thought, a strange sensation overtook Iamelichos. He felt as if he had entered another world, a world of peace and tranquillity. The sweet delight of trust in God tingled in all the fibres of his being. Material words could never describe such a sensation. *How strange!* he wondered. *How did the prophets ever talk to their kin?*

Words were pounding onto his heart. No, not words

— but wordless meanings. Unbidden, these shining words came tumbling out of his mouth. '*Now that you have turned away from all that these people worship other than God, seek refuge in the cave. Your God will shower his mercy upon you and quell your distress.*'

A strange spirituality radiated from him, and none doubted his words. It was as if God himself were inviting them to the cave. Iamelichos' secret delight spread into their hearts, which overflowed with peace and love towards God.

It was unlike any other feeling they knew, not even the love they had for their children. Perhaps this was another matter that humankind had no words for.

'I will accompany you,' Antonios announced.

'You? Why?' Maximilian asked in astonishment.

'In order to be with you.'

Dionysios did not allow any more objections. 'Then we will be on our way tonight.'

'We cannot wait until nightfall,' warned Maximilian. 'We left many traces in the wild. Someone might have seen us. The guards could be here before dusk.'

'But they will see us if we leave now.'

'Most of the men have gone to the fields,' considered Antonios, 'and the women are still at home. We cannot leave all at once, but if we leave one by one, we will attract the least attention.'

The others nodded in agreement.

'I will go to the sheep owners now and tell them I am unable to take their sheep out today. I will be back by the time you have finished your tea.'

Soon, they set out, keeping several stones' throw between them. True to Antonios' word, the dusty streets were nearly deserted. Circumventing the shady vineries and olive groves, they lightly ascended the foothills until they met halfway up the slopes, well out of sight of the village.

It was now midmorning. Fear, exhaustion, and lack of food had taken their toll on them, and they sank down against a giant rock for a brief rest.

Suddenly, something rustled in the foliage. Leaping up, Maximilian seized a stick and took a couple steps forward. The others glanced around nervously. They had no weapons, and they were completely exposed.

Out sprung a giant golden brown dog. Wagging its tail, it bounded onto Antonios and began licking his feet and hands.

'Comteri!' Antonios chided, as the others sighed in relief. 'Go home!'

Drooping his ears, the dog gazed at him forlornly.

'Go home!' repeated Antonios. 'Go! Go!'

Sadly, Comteri stood for a moment and then wandered towards a distant mountain stream.

'We have lingered here too long,' cautioned Maximilian. 'Next time, we might not be so fortunate.'

Setting aside their weariness, they took to the slopes again. Just as they moved, however, a distinctive brown blur came running towards them.

'I don't understand,' moaned Antonios. 'He's usually such an obedient dog.' Petting the dog affectionately, he firmly repeated his command. 'Go home, Comteri. Go home.'

It was as if Comteri wanted to tell them something. With a pained expression, Antonios picked up a round mountain stone and hurled it at Comteri's legs. Comteri refused to budge.

'Do you think he will betray us?' asked Martinos, who was less comfortable with canines.

'He is a clever and, normally, obedient dog,' apologized Antonios. 'He might help us.'

'It's getting late,' Maximilian reminded them. 'Dog or no dog, they will find us if we remain here too long. We'd best move on.'

Rapidly, the slopes grew steeper as they approached the cave. Their feet began to slip on the ground, and, at one point, they had to clutch at the rocks for support.

They had almost reached the peak when Iamelichos pulled aside a leafy branch and revealed the hidden entrance to the cave. It was indeed, as Iamelichos had described it, perfect.

Gratefully, they sheltered themselves inside this natural wonder. A beautiful serenity emanated from the chiselled walls — no doubt, the remnant of Iamelichos' elaborate prayers.

Making himself at home on the broad overhang, Maximilian spread out their provisions. 'Let's eat,' he declared. 'I'm famished.'

None could argue. Forming a circle around the cloth, they partook in their small meal. The tiny bundle of food could hardly replenish their strength, but, in this wondrous home, it seemed like a godsend.

As soon as they had finished, Iamelichos raised his hands to the cave roof. 'We thank thee, O Lord, for your kind sustenance and your promised safety. Amen.'

'Amen,' the others repeated.

Martinos had a quizzical look on his face. 'How strange that when we set out, we were not mindful of how to obtain food or water. We could stay here for quite a while.'

'We did not choose this cave,' Iamelichos affirmed with absolute certainty. 'God has invited us, and we are his guests. So let us see what our host has prepared for us.'

'All people are God's guests,' added Maximilian, 'though most realize it not. If they did, they would never worry. They would trust in their host and welcome whatever he provided.'

'But most people have to work to earn a living,' objected Dionysios. 'Their sustenance is not just handed to them.'

'We gather our sustenance by working. But we do not produce it. God creates our sustenance, measures it, and provides it. What can a farmer do but plant the seeds and wait? Only those who are not mindful of God are anxious about the morrow.'

'When their hearts find God,' added Iamelichos, 'they become serene.'

Joannes spoke up. 'Judah always used to say: If tomorrow is not to be a part of our life, thinking about tomorrow's sustenance is futile. If tomorrow is to be a part of our life, then we shall taste its sustenance. Alas, would he were still with us.'

The six fell silent in remembrance of him.

Dionysios examined Iamelichos thoughtfully. 'I feel like you and your friends understand God better than us.' Iamelichos smiled humbly. 'We have a question that has long been eating away at our hearts.'

'I can try to help,' promised Iamelichos.

'Our question is: why does falsehood always overpower truth? Why doesn't God make truth victorious? Why doesn't he bring a great sign that will end all doubt?'

'God has gifted us with free will,' answered Iamelichos. 'Without free will, we would never be able to reach our most exalted accomplishments. Unfortunately, some destroy themselves with their free will like a soldier who kills himself with his own sword.'

'But are they not transgressing the will of God?'

'God has promised to bring victory to truth in the end,' replied Iamelichos. 'I believe his promise. However, I too have not witnessed this come to pass, and so I rely upon God's grace to help me keep my faith. But I can tell you what I have witnessed.'

Carefully, Dionysios and his friends listened as Iamelichos laid out the parable with his hands, just as Judah would have done. 'Have you seen the rain which God pours down from the clouds? It flows in torrents across the lands. As the water rushes by, frothy foam rises to the top and hides the water beneath. All you see is the foam. But, soon, the foam vanishes, and the pure water remains.

'This is our story. The falsehood will soon wash away, and the truth will remain. God has willed us to have free choice and has promised to requite us for our deeds. But all we see now is the froth – the reign of falsehood, the vanity of these people. It will soon perish.'

'We cannot comprehend God's will within our own lifetimes,' added Maximilian. 'Time has no meaning for God. Granting these tyrants respite means nothing to him. All we can do is have faith that this too shall come to pass.'

'I believe you,' said Exakoustodianos. 'But my heart wishes to witness this within our own lifetimes so that it can solidify its certainty.' Then he prayed, 'O God! Send down your mercy upon us, and prepare us for what is to come.'

'Amen,' they repeated again.

'I am glad I am with you,' murmured Antonios, glowing, and Dionysios regarded him warmly.

Rising, Joannes peered out from the mouth of the cave. 'No one is in sight,' he reported. 'We should rest a bit, lest fatigue overwhelm us.' And then he stretched himself out on the large flat rock. The others did the same. The stone was hard, and the cave cold, but none of the noblemen noticed.

There were six of them, and Antonios made seven. Forgotten, Comteri rested outside. Altogether, they numbered eight, and the eighth was their dog.

What could they have been thinking of as they drifted off to sleep? Their families? The soldiers? God?

No one really knows what thoughts drifted through their minds as they embarked upon their long slumber. All that can be said is that they soon fell into a very deep sleep.

PART TWO

XII

THE ARREST

While Sanctus stationed his men all across town, Diocletian's emissaries sped across the countryside under the shadow of night to enlist the aid of the neighbouring security forces. At first light, soldiers began crawling the lands. Abandoned huts, suspicious buildings, lopsided granaries – nothing was left untouched. There would be no second escape.

Bitterly, Diocletian escorted the Emperor to the gates with subdued fanfare. Although the Emperor seemed to put the situation in more perspective, Diocletian was still in shock. The past night had transcended his wildest fears.

As Diocletian retreated to his palace, he sensed that the people were talking in the streets. The once forbidden subject of Christianity had exploded. Merchants who had hitherto regarded Christianity as the religion of cloth-weavers and carpet-makers now clustered around each others' stalls and debated it. The more thoughtful – who had once deigned it beneath their dignity to run the word over their tongues – now began contemplating the principles of Christian belief. Everywhere, the once fearful Christians now carried themselves with newfound pride. Such wise and eminent men had been Christians, just like them! The occasional Christian oath began to slip out just within earshot of Diocletian's men, infuriating them.

But anxiety tempered excitement for the fugitives' kith and kin. Anna had been the first to bring the news of the escape to the other families. Together, they prayed daily for their husbands to reach a safe haven while Gallus kept them all continually updated, retelling each rumour like an epic tale dominated by the exploits of his wise and magnanimous master.

Gallus never ran short of material, for the rumours had multiplied. The glass-blowers said the men had escaped into Byzantium. The perfumers swore they had disappeared into Arabia. The bookbinders calculated they had taken to the Mediterranean Sea. And the credulous told everything else.

As the days turned into weeks, and the weeks turned into months, the families began to build up hope against hope. Then, one morning like any other morning, the palace convoy trekked past a nondescript collection of hovels. In what was now a routine procedure, Sanctus' men broke off to question the villagers.

But what happened next was far from routine. As the soldiers paraded their grandiose steeds through the nonexistent roads, a young farmer reported that, a week or so after the Festival of Mars, he had seen several strange men sneaking out of Antonios' home. Intrigued, he had shadowed them all the way out to the fields, whereupon they had disappeared into the heart of Mount Angelos, never to be seen again.

Sceptically, the soldiers conferred among themselves. This was not the first desperate soul to have come seeking a reward. But then, a wood-chopper came forward and confessed that he had seen six men traipsing up the slopes with a shepherd and his dog — 'spoiling their fine gowns on the thorns, but I durst not speak it, lest they reckon I imbibed the wine.'

Before long, waves of soldiers swarmed the mountain from all sides as the villagers looked on in amazement. Most of them had never seen the Roman war machine in full force before.

By late afternoon, however, the soldiers had still found no trace of the renegades, and they were beginning to tire.

'Sir,' advised Matius, 'I doubt they are here. Even if they had been up here, they would have fled down the other side by now.'

'No,' swore Sanctus. 'Where could they have gone? I wager they are hiding between the folds of these very rocks. We will search the mountain to its peak. They will not escape.'

Discouraged, Matius continued trudging up the mountain. At least, once they reached the summit, they would be done.

Suddenly, Sanctus halted. 'Matius!' he shouted,

pointing off in the distance. 'A dog!'

Matius had no idea what Sanctus was pointing to, but he followed Sanctus as he trampled the herbage in pursuit of his goal. Soon, he realized Sanctus was right; it was a dog. A satisfied grin spread across Sanctus' face. But his expression soon sobered as they neared the dog: the sleeping dog was absolutely and utterly terrifying.

The dog seemed like it had come straight out of a Greek myth. Matius eyed it as if it were Cerberus, the three-headed dog who supposedly guarded the underworld. He wanted to bolt. Finally, Sanctus yelled, 'Spearmen!'

In any other circumstances, it would have sounded ludicrous. But here, on the edge of Mount Angelos, they jumped at his command, and several soldiers uneasily surrounded the fearsome dog. It did not move at all, and that was some comfort. But its eyes were wide open, as if it were staring into their souls.

Keeping a healthy distance between himself and the dog, Sanctus surveyed the terrain. By now, their footprints would have been spoiled. But ashes, bent branches, refuse – they must have left some tracks. Just as he was about to give up hope, he found it. An overgrown oak branch had been disturbed. Snapping it aside, he beheld a vast blackness leading into the rock.

'Torch!' he yelled. Quickly, a soldier brought him a flaming brand. It dispelled none of the darkness, but the fugitives need not know that. 'Come out!' he demanded. 'You cannot hide!'

His own voice echoed weakly back to him. At

Sanctus' signal, Matius and two guards forged ahead while Sanctus strained to read the cave's innards.

Suddenly, Matius fled past him, screaming. The others came clambering after him. Ignoring Sanctus, they sped down the rocky slope and collapsed into a heap well away from the cave.

Sanctus sprinted after them. 'What happened?'

Shivering, Matius opened his mouth but spoke no words. The others were completely dazed.

'Matius!' yelled Sanctus. He shook him vigorously. 'Matius! What happened? Matius!'

'Ss-sir!' stuttered Matius unnaturally. 'Sir! It was horrible. H-h-horrible!'

'What? What was horrible?'

'Ss-sir, t-they were in the c-cave. It was horrible, sir!'

'Talk sense,' Sanctus demanded. 'Don't just keep saying *horrible*.'

'T-they didn't move, sir. Their eyes here horrible. They were staring at us!' Sanctus was staring, too. 'T-they were dead. No, alive. No, asleep – no, awake. And they were staring at us….'

Sanctus was floored. Matius was one of his best soldiers, and he had never seen him this frightened before. Matius' fear robbed him of his own courage. Climbing back up the rocks, he positioned himself safely outside the cave. 'Come out!' he demanded. 'You cannot escape!'

Nothing happened. Defeated, Sanctus returned to his subordinates. 'The darkness is affecting our minds,' he muttered. 'We will stay here and arrest them at sunup.'

He beckoned for a runner. 'You. Make haste for Philadelphia and inform the palace that the fugitives have been captured. We will return them to town tomorrow.'

'Yes, sir,' assented the messenger before nimbly working his way down the rocky inclines.

A score of guards kept watch over the cave, lighting so many torches that the villagers thought there was a fire. Eventually, however, the soldiers stared to ignore the dog. It had not moved once, and so they assumed it was dead. No one paused to consider that the vultures circling above did not get near it.

Although he was not usually an early riser, Sanctus awoke at the sun's first pallid rays. Hoisting himself from the bumpy ground, he grabbed his sword and headed for the cave. As the tired guards saluted, he stared inside. The cave was facing south, and the sun was in the east. He waited. But although the sun rose swiftly above the trees, he still could not quite tell what was in the cave.

Wielding his sword, Sanctus reluctantly entered the cave. Times like this were when he disliked being a commander. Surveying left and right, he edged forward. Suddenly, his feet gave way, and he found himself dashing for the exit. Horror subsumed him, and he thought he might retch. He kept running and running. He was sure he had lost them, but, brandishing his sword, he turned back to the cave to make sure.

Matius ducked out of reach of the blade. 'Did you

see them, sir?'

Panting, Sanctus sank down onto the rocks. 'Yes. It is dreadful, Matius. Dreadful. I think they are dead.'

'Sir, they don't seem to be dead. They don't even seem to be asleep. It's like they're going to pounce.'

Sanctus nodded and swallowed heavily. 'But they have not moved, so they must be dead.'

'Sir, even if they are dead, the soldiers cannot bring them out. They would drop their swords in fear.'

'Strange,' mused Sanctus. 'I have never seen such a thing until now.'

'Me neither,' agreed Matius. 'What are we going to do? We told Diocletian we arrested them.'

'I will speak to Diocletian myself,' volunteered Sanctus stoically. Matius did not envy him. 'You take over guard.'

'Yes, sir.'

As Sanctus departed, Matius heard him muttering, 'They are dead, they have to be dead.' He sounded as if he were trying to convince himself.

'This is ridiculous!' Diocletian reprimanded him. 'Has their insanity infected you?'

'Excellency, believe me,' Sanctus replied, flustered. 'Send someone to see for yourself. Our most courageous men could not get near them.'

'What a brave army,' Diocletian censured him. 'Good news for Philadelphia!'

Sanctus sighed. He had not expected any other response. 'Excellency, I am sure they are dead. They have not moved since nightfall. Perhaps they died in some dreadful way. Their eyes are wide open.' As much as he tried to hide it, fear crept into his voice. 'It's like they're going to attack.'

'Gods in Olympia,' muttered Diocletian.

'Believe me,' swore Sanctus. 'I entered the cave myself. I was out so fast I didn't even have time to get scared.'

Uncharacteristically, Diocletian held his tongue. Sanctus was a seasoned commander. His six closest counsellors had escaped with a shepherd, and now they were terrorizing his soldiers. He was losing his populace. Rome was dissatisfied. He didn't need any more problems.

'Very well,' he concluded. 'Don't force them out.'

'Excellency?' repeated Sanctus.

'Block them in there. It can be their grave.'

Pleased that Diocletian had not asked him to re-enter the cave, Sanctus bowed and turned to leave.

'Wait!' called Diocletian. Sanctus turned back. The lines in his face seemed more pronounced. 'Give them an ultimatum first. That is – if they are not already dead.'

Matius twiddled his thumbs, hoping Diocletian had not put Sanctus to a bad end. Just then, he heard a familiar heavy footfall. He ran over to the groves. 'How was the meeting, Sir?'

Sanctus smiled, and Matius felt a sense of relief. Together, they headed for the cave's entrance, whereupon Sanctus yelled, 'Excellency Maximilianos!

Excellency Iamelichos! Can you hear me?'

They stood in the mountain silence. Sanctus was no longer smiling. 'His Highness Diocletian has ordered me to block the cave. Can you hear me? I have orders to close up the cave. Come out, or you will be buried alive.'

As before, nothing happened. Feigning indifference, Sanctus shrugged his shoulders. 'You heard the order.' Then he turned away and wandered towards the edge of the clearing, mumbling again, 'They must be dead.' He did not speculate on how they might have died.

Diligently, Matius formed teams of soldiers. Together, they gathered stones, prepared mortar, and laid the wall. Before long, the makeshift wall had – more or less – isolated the cave.

With puffy eyes, Sanctus inspected it. Uneven gaps dotted the top of the wall, allowing a draft in and out. Sanctus did not care. So what if the corpses got cold. His men were soldiers, not masons, and they were overstrained. If the counsellors weren't dead already, they soon would be, and Philadelphia's finest noblemen would take their eternal rest in Mount Angelos. Diocletian was leaving a fine legacy for himself.

Turning away, he ordered, 'Break camp!' Gratefully, the soldiers headed down towards the countryside. No one really wanted to spend any more time near the cave than necessary. He pulled aside Matius. 'Keep up a guard. Don't let their sympathizers break down the wall.'

'Yes, sir,' replied Matius dutifully.

Again, the villagers stared in astonishment at how

efficiently the Philadelphian presence vacated Raqim.
After a day or so, life returned to normal.

Meanwhile, hidden inside their cave, Iamelichos and
his friends shifted in their sleep, oblivious to the events
unfolding outside.

XIII

THE MARTYRS

The verdict struck like thunder. The execution was not a trifle. Unfettered by the city walls, the tale spread far into the neighbouring lands. *Diocletian's top counsellors became Christian. They denied the deities and defied the Emperor then ran off under the commander's nose. Diocletian's soldiers were too coward to arrest them so they buried them alive in a cave.*

Although under threat of death, the faithful met almost every night to come up with a solution, their hopes of finding the men alive diminished with every passing day. With few men and fewer weapons, they could not take on the guards. Had they been certain the men were alive, some might have tried. But no one had reported a single sign of life. They were certain, however, that if they so much as laid a finger on the guards, Diocletian and his army could lean back and relax as Philadelphia's pagan zealots took care of them.

They began to console one another with the all-too-common words: *We did what we could.* Every week, in their secret pre-dawn prayer ceremonies, they mentioned the names of these exalted and freedom-loving men along with Judah's for a poignant moment of silence. The past was bitter, and the future did not portend well.

Not knowing was worst of all. Maria only prayed that the men had died before their confinement. Since that fateful night, Gallus had not smiled once, and a strange sorrow now parched his lined face. Iamelichos had not simply been his master. He had been his hero — his inspiration and his ideal. Although Iamelichos could not have met a more heroic death, Gallus could not bear it, and it showed.

Too young to understand the hows and whys of the situation, the children constantly asked for their fathers. No one knew what to say. How could anyone tell them their fathers had been buried — probably alive — in a cave — and could still be dying? Since that day, the children had not even been let out of the house, lest their friends inform them of the horrifying fate that had cut short their fathers' lives.

But the children were not stupid, and the grown-ups were not that self-restrained while discussing this issue around them.

A couple weeks later, Maria had been absently having breakfast with her son when, half-eaten loaf in hand, he informed her, 'Mother! Father is probably dead by now.'

Maria stared at Archimedes' childish and innocent face. Tears filled her eyes as she wracked her brain for a reassuring yet truthful response

'I heard that people die after ten days of no food. Father has no food. The soldiers won't let anyone bring them food.'

Maria's attempts to restrain herself fell short, and she began to sob.

'Mother! Can we take some food for him? Do you know where his cave is?'

Controlling herself with difficulty, she replied, 'Son, your father no longer needs food. He is with God. God gives him better things.'

Archimedes was listening carefully.

'Son, you must be proud of your father. He was a hero, killed for Jesus and for God. He did his duty. You must always try to be like him.'

Maria's words were branded onto Archimedes' brain like scalding lead poured into a mould. Archimedes safeguarded these words for a lifetime like an etching on a costly gem as he struggled with the hardships of life as a Christian.

As the days wore on, their flames of hope dimmed. The children were told that their fathers were martyred on the path of God. Proudly, they narrated the tale to their friends. No longer did anyone have plans to break down the wall. Gradually, all talk of braving the terror of the cave in order to retrieve their remains faded. The city's Christians began to accept that these men would never return and felt that their final resting place should be respected. If God had decreed that they should end their earthly journey there, who were they to question him?

After a month of dead silence, Diocletian recalled his guards and ordered a copper plaque to be hung above the cave as a deterrent to all citizens – present and future. It read:

HERE LIE MAXIMILIANVS IAMBLICHVS MARTINVS EXAKVTODIANVS DIONYSIVS AND IOANNES THE PALACE COVNSELLORS OF PHILADELPHIA. THEY CONVERTED TO THE FALSE RELIGION OF JESVS OF NAZARETH AND REFVSED TO WORSHIP THE EMPEROR. THE EMPEROR'S TRIVMPHANT FORCES BVRIED THEM ALIVE IN THIS CAVE.

HIS HIGHNESS DIOCLETIAN
DCCCLXXXIII AB VRBE CONDITA

The court historians also documented the events in the volumes describing Emperor Hadrian's era. The head copyist – who had a secret leaning towards Christianity – recorded the heroic story with utmost diligence so it would not fade from the pages of history. He was the only one to mention Antonios' name in the account; as far as the others were concerned, only six men of import had been killed. He then etched the tale onto a tablet of silver and secured it in the palace treasury, ostensibly as part of the royal wealth.

Over time, fresh tragedies and the monotony of daily life erased their memory from the people's minds. It has always been thus: the new conquers the old. Nothing remained but another bitter memory for the Christians, an exciting story for the Philadelphians, a political challenge for Diocletian, and a heroic memory for their survivors. Weakened by the wind and rain, the makeshift wall soon crumbled, but the army always came up with excuses why they should not build it again. No one really liked getting near the cave. Those who dared to climb up to it fled in such terror that they diluted others' desire to make the tedious journey, and the frozen figures faded into legend.

Meanwhile, the men shifted in their sleep, oblivious to the events unfolding outside. Like a powerful ward, the sleeping dog lay soundly on his rock, and even other animals kept away. Few noticed him, however, not even the rare souls who tiptoed up there, only to scramble back down in terror.

XIV

THE RETURN

Maria and Archimedes gazed up at the new portrait in the sitting room. A Syriac man named Hashim had painted it from memory and offered it to them as his own expression of grief. In it, Iamelichos seemed even more shining and noble than he had been in life. Archimedes was fascinated; it was as if he could see his father whom he had not seen for years. But Maria needed no portrait; she still remembered her husband every day, and the image only pained her.

Suddenly, Gallus burst in. 'Hadrian is dead!'

Archimedes leaped up with childish joy. His worst memory in life was entwined with Hadrian. 'Really?'

'The Senate has designated his stepson Antonius as the new Emperor.'

'What difference does it make?' Maria chided him.

'My lady, the people have hailed him Antonius the Pious. He is an ascetic man. He is not like his predecessor.'

Maria raised her eyebrows dubiously.

'Of course,' clarified Gallus, 'he accepted the title reluctantly. But, perhaps, he might spare our blood and tolerate our beliefs and permit our ceremonies.'

'Speaking pious words is not a sign of piety,' Maria reproved him. 'An ascetic does not take back with his hands what he kicked away with his feet. Since when has the Senate been a bedfellow with the pious?'

'My lady!'

'Antonius, I have heard, is pious only towards his own gods. We should expect harsher times.'

'But...'

'But what? We don't lack religious freedom. Thousands of foreign gods are right at home here. Religious fanaticism is not the problem. Imperial fanaticism is. I am sure Antonius will be just as dedicated to keeping his position as the former Emperors. This is the root of our troubles.'

Gallus lowered his head. Since childhood, Maria had seen nothing but murder, torture, and tragedy for the Christians. After her husband had been buried alive, she had lost interest in affairs of state. The light of hope no longer shone in her heart.

'The Empire fears us, Gallus. The other religions adopt their falsehoods under the pretext of belief. But we are a threat. We topple their godheads and fight their swords with our necks. Do you think it is a coincidence that Nero blamed us for the great fire in Rome? Or that Domitian passed a law against us simply on a whim?' She sighed. 'Do you really believe Antonius will leave us alone?

In all honesty, he didn't, but Hadrian's demise was still good news. Just then, he noticed the portrait. A smile crossed his eyes, and Archimedes grinned back at him. Putting on an air of seriousness, he asked, 'You are ready, Master Archimedes?'

Archimedes nodded. For months, Archimedes had been begging his mother to let Gallus take him to the cave. Finally, she had relented, and Archimedes still could not believe he was going to visit the mountain. To him, Mount Angelos was not just a mountain; it was a wish come true.

Gallus had warned him that they could not approach the cave, but everyone had their own reasons why. The Christians whispered that God had rewarded them for their heroic martyrdom. The pagans said that the gods had inflicted their wrath upon them by keeping others from burying them. Julian just saw it as a sign of the times and lowered his head as he went about his business. But Archimedes could not understand any of these explanations. Surely, his father could not be that frightening?

Soon, they left, and the bored guards ignored them as they drove their carriage south from the Philadelphian gates. The road was nearly empty, and stalks of grain waved in the warm summer breeze.

As usual, Archimedes bombarded Gallus with questions. Although Gallus had become his mentor and taught him to become a man, Gallus' exciting stories still let Archimedes look to his father as a role model.

Indeed, Archimedes had a peculiar understanding for a child of his age. In that regard, he was not unlike his father.

'Master Archimedes!' Gallus suddenly cried out. 'Mount Angelos!'

The dry brown mountain crowned with crisp green foliage plunged Archimedes into sweet memories of the past. Seeing Angelos was like seeing his father, and his eyes overflowed with tears. It was as if his father were here with him now, holding his small hands and narrating words of wisdom in the guise of children's stories.

The mountain invited them closer until they could drive no more, at which point they began to climb, Archimedes bounding up the steep slopes. The awaited summit grew closer and closer until, finally, Gallus called out breathlessly, 'Master Archimedes! Do you see it?'

An unforgettable sensation filled Archimedes, one he knew he could never explain. It was as if he were part of that great mountain which had become part and parcel of his father's epic. 'Can we go inside?' he asked in half-excitement, half-trepidation.

'Absolutely not. It is completely impossible.' Gallus' voice had a hint of fear.

'Are you sure?'

'I am sure.' Gallus had never told anyone, but he had once ventured inside the cave. He had never gone back.

Contented, Archimedes sat down on a rock and explored the cave with his eyes. He could just make out the crumbling wall. Had they approached further, they could have seen the macabre figures, but Gallus did not want to leave Archimedes with that memory of his father.

The sun crossed overhead, and he felt Gallus' hand on his shoulder. 'We'd better go back, Master Archimedes.'

Archimedes had not tired of looking. He could have sat there forever. He wanted to lie down and become one with the earth that had taken his father. It was the first place he had ever felt a real connection with him. But, obediently, he rose, locking the cave in his memory and wishing his sentiments to his father with all his heart. It would only be the first of many trips he would eventually make to the cave.

Meanwhile, Iamelichos and his friends shifted in their sleep, oblivious to the events unfolding outside.

They passed the Temple of Mithras on their way home. An import goddess, Mithras had been Persia's dubious gift to the Roman possessions. Her priests were now baptizing their latest initiates in the open temple courtyard. Since Archimedes had never seen this ceremony before, Gallus stopped the carriage so he could watch.

Several brawny priests shoved a heavy iron grate off a pit. After the novices disappeared down it, they pushed the grate back on. The novices were locked in. Several other muscular priests dragged a bull onto the pit. Stubbornly, the bull reared back at them — even though the priests were built like bulls themselves. Together, the priests forced it down, and one of them seized a dagger and deftly slashed its throat. Like all its other four-legged friends, it had been conquered, and, as its life blood drained away, a priest in a brown tunic chanted incomprehensible verses. As soon as the flow had slowed to a trickle, the priests heaved the carcass aside. Bathed in blood, the devotees climbed out.

Archimedes had been staring so hard that he had not blinked once. 'Do they worship Cybele?'

'No, Mithras.'

'But you said that Cybele's worshippers baptise themselves in bull's blood.'

'They do that too.'

Gallus spurred on the horses, and soon they arrived safely home. At the sound of their carriage wheels, Maria rushed out and enfolded Archimedes in her arms, inwardly wincing as Archimedes eagerly chattered about the cave.

However, that day remained frozen in his mind for years – the years in which he had to somehow grow and flourish in such a society. A society baptised in blood would have no gift for its adversaries but blood.

XV

THE PHILOSOPHER
KING

C urled up beneath Iamelichos' portrait, Archimedes
was perusing one of his father's manuscripts. From
time to time, he stroked the hair of his four year old
child Elias who was resting sleepily upon him.

Suddenly, Gallus burst in with as much speed as he
could muster. 'Excellency Archimedes! Antonius is dead!
The Senate has designated Marcus Aurelius as his
successor.' He leaned on the divan, trying to catch his
breath.

Archimedes recalled what his mother had said over
two decades ago. No doubt, she would have said the
same, had God not taken her to his mercy. But he
beamed. 'Marcus Aurelius the philosopher. Things have
turned out to Aristotle's satisfaction!'

In true Carthaginian style, Gallus danced around a
bit, even though he was still out of breath. 'I feel simply

jubilant. I'd like to celebrate tonight.'

'Me too,' admitted Archimedes, 'but only because another one of Satan's henchman has been removed from this world. We can't expect any improvements. We can only pray that things don't get worse.' His voice grew more serious. 'We have a duty to perform. The changing faces of the Emperor have nothing to do with us.' Gently moving Elias aside, he retrieved a small scroll from the cedar desk he had inherited and stamped it with a big wax seal. 'The messenger needs to deliver this letter to the Bishop of Antioch. It is absolutely confidential.'

As Gallus clasped the letter in his wrinkled hands, Archimedes quietly informed him, 'I am going to see Joseph.' Joseph had become a second Judah until Cassius — Diocletian's successor — had issued the order for his arrest, even though Cassius was much less sensitive about Christians than Diocletian had been. Preoccupied with grander issues, he ignored the riffraff's theological sensitivities — so long as they stayed in line. Unfortunately, Joseph had crossed the line.

Just as adamantly, Archimedes took it upon himself to protect Joseph. Truth be told, he now battled on two fronts. On the external front, he fought against the Roman rulers and the devotees of Jupiter and Mithras. As he tirelessly organized his brethren, he was a constant witness to fear, imprisonment, and murder as, one by one, his friends were plucked away. Someday, his turn would also arrive. Of course, depending on the governor's whims, the repression waxed and waned. But

Archimedes had never seen a time when doomed owl of torture, trouble, and injustice had slept.

Inside the mission, he struggled to repair the cracks that had been hewn into the solid wall of monotheistic belief. He tried to crush the seeds which Satan had hatched in the warmth of people's hearts. However, he met nothing but disappointment. Forcing himself to remember that they were all followers of Jesus, he selflessly put his life on the line, side by side with his brethren who had lost their way. With a pure heart, he strode forward on the path to truth.

Furtively, Archimedes glanced up and down the decrepit lane. The door in front of him had no lock, and, carefully, he pushed it open. The one-room shack was on the verge of collapse, and even the poor were afraid to live in it.

'It's me, Archimedes,' he whispered.

A scrawny man with a ruddy beard crawled out from a dusty corner, and Archimedes handed over the parcel of food. 'You shouldn't have troubled yourself,' Joseph murmured gracefully.

'Gallus was busy tonight.'

'You put me to shame.'

'No, not at all. I have other business too. I have arranged for you to leave Philadelphia with the messenger.'

'Leave? Why should I leave?'

'Your life is in danger. You will not last long here.'

'Let them come. Death is sweet.'

'It is not important what is sweet,' Archimedes reproved him. 'It is important for you to do your duty, and your duty is to live. You will accompany the Bishop of Antioch to another city where you can start your work anew. Is that not better than being caught.'

Joseph was pensive. 'You think it is better this way?'

'Certainly,' Archimedes replied, this time his voice full of affection. 'You want God's approval, right? I am sure this will meet with his approval.'

Joseph still looked grim, but a flicker of hope shone in his eyes. 'Tonight, at eight o'clock, you will leave,' Archimedes told him.

'Thank you, Archimedes. You truly are a fine brother.'

Archimedes embraced Joseph. 'May God be with you. May God always help you.' They parted, and Archimedes took one last look at the illustrious preacher. 'The messenger is a good and experienced man. He knows where to take you. Heed his word.'

Joseph's eyes remained fixated on the door even after Archimedes had left. He could not imagine how he would begin his life again in a strange land. He had to have faith that God intended to give him a second chance.

Suddenly, the door burst open. 'Joseph! The soldiers! Someone has betrayed you!'

Joseph stared, incomprehensively. Archimedes grabbed him, and they ran, a squadron of soldiers chasing them on foot. In their wake, citizens locked themselves behind doors, and onlookers stared out windows. It was to no avail.

'Let's split up,' Archimedes panted. 'Eight o'clock in the cemetery.' The soldiers swarmed behind them.

Instinctively, Archimedes wended his way through the alleyways he had known since childhood. With a stroke of luck, he found himself right next to the Temple of Cybele. Today was her festival. Bowing his head, he lost himself in the throngs of worshippers entering the temple. Thick smoke from the candles and incense had darkened the interior, and the crowd pressed around him. He could not have left even if he had wanted to. Coughing, he decided to wait it out.

An influential goddess, Cybele had imposed her will all across the Empire for thousands of years. On this day, the demigod Attis was said to have immolated himself under a pine tree in atonement for hurting her. As his blood dripped down, his soul fled into the tree, and violets sprung up from the droplets. In a re-enactment of the scene, a great pine tree had been dragged down from the mountains and draped in violets; the sharp scent of its needles cut through the musty incense. Around it, priests clad in pitch black robes mourned the loss of Attis and hit each other's heads and bodies with wooden sticks.

After the priests had given each other a proper beating, they cast their sticks aside and sat on the floor. Acolytes brought them goblets filled to the brim with sacrificial blood. They drank up, and, as if crazed by inebriating wine, ripped off the black robes and began jumping up and down. As they slashed themselves with daggers drawn from their waistbands, blood spattered across the temple and garbed the priests in red. Attis' lifeless body had been purified, and his resurrection would be soon.

Archimedes felt ill. Why were humans in need of such spiritual intoxication? Why did they love these frenzied outbursts? Why did humans often struggle in vain to resist this temptation – even thought was a base and false need?

Why had humans always wanted to create gods for themselves? These gods had no prophets, no message, no reason for their existence. Had they lost themselves trying to find God? What was this love that blazed inside them at a sight of a woman? It burned every fibre and removed every thought of the Beloved, replacing the flame that should always burn for God.

It was a pity that humans did not give this love – this great power and miracle of old – the chance to manifest itself and flourish. Instead, they wasted it on meagre matters like lust, wealth, and the divinities. They squandered this capital cheaply on goods that would never be delivered.

Love is your only capital, Jesus had said. Archimedes had heard these words so often it was as if he had been there to hear them himself. Beware not to purchase base thoughts with your love, as you will find no profit. Your thoughts, words, and actions must all be for God. Only in this will you find peace.

What was worship but love? Human beings had no task more vital than deciding whom to direct this primal love towards. All prophets had come to assist them in that choice so that the capital of their existence – their love and affection – would not be squandered on the trifling goods of this world. Alas, how cheaply most humans sold it.

As Archimedes waited, the priests settled themselves back on the bloodied floor, exhausted. Their task was not yet through. They had to bathe and renew their spiritual fervour for the resurrection and ascension which was scheduled for the day after tomorrow – Sunday.

Some of his fellow Christians had taken to preaching the same thing. Archimedes now understood the true import of his father's words: *These people have mistaken Christianity for the Roman religions. In return for the Romans' willingness to accept their God, the Christian preachers compromised Jesus to the Roman godheads.*

Sensing that danger was no longer lurking outside, Archimedes slipped from the temple. Dusk was approaching, and the streets were now deserted. He did not yet know that Joseph had been caught.

Sending such a great catch straight to prison would have been such a tremendous waste, so the police chief brought Joseph to Cassius personally. Of course, the chief had already plied Cassius' ears with pompous overstatements of Joseph's importance, until Cassius wondered if the chief thought he had arrested Jesus himself.

Now, at a signal from the guards, his soldiers dragged Joseph before Cassius' throne. Joseph's tattered clothes and bloodied torso told of a hard struggle during the arrest.

Cassius approached the frail, bloodied prisoner with a devilish smirk. 'So you are Joseph the missionary. A pity. You had attained quite some fame for yourself.'

Joseph stared at the floor.

'Why silent? You are a real talker. Why don't you pray for the God of Jesus to save you? Or, should I say, the God of the weak and wretched. Could it be that he is feeble and miserable, just like his servants?'

The attendants unanimously and obediently burst into laughter. Joseph remained silent.

Cassius unsheathed his sword. 'If he could, he would have protected his son.' Face to face with Joseph, he etched a bloody cross on his chest. 'What a meek boy! He died on the cross. Poor lad!'

As he sliced the sword deeper into Joseph's flesh, Joseph crumpled to the floor. The soldiers hauled him back up.

'Regretful?' Cassius mocked him. 'Do you want to repent?'

'God has no son,' Joseph whispered weakly. 'You depict God in your own image and give him a wife and son. God is free from human characteristics. God – '

'Enough. Even here, you start preaching? You truly are stubborn. Take him away.'

'Sir,' asked the chief, 'should we take him to court?'

'Ah, how finicky you are,' reproached Cassius. 'He

needs no court.'

'Then what is your command?'

'They say Christians are extremely kind-hearted — just like their God. Or else, their God is just like them, I don't know.' Slowly, the evil smile returned. 'The lions are hungry, and I am sure his Excellency Joseph is generous enough to feed them.' He ran the edge of his sword across Joseph's bare flesh. 'Is that not right?'

'For the enemies of God, we have naught but wrath and rage.'

Cassius rounded on him. 'Shut up!'

The commander stepped in. 'Take him away,' he directed. Joseph was dragged out, leaving a bloody trail.

'I don't know when their God will come to their aid,' Cassius muttered. 'How obstinate they are!'

'You will understand when you die, Cassius!' Joseph shouted back with all his might. 'You will no longer have a hold on this world. You will see your past life as a flash of cruelty that can never be brought back. Cassius! . . . '

Joseph's voice was silenced.

They took him to the amphitheatre. Games were already scheduled for that night, and the crowd fell mute at this unexpected surprise. It had been some time since Christians had been thrown to the lions.

In the sandy arena, Joseph stood alone. As he waited for death, he raised his head to the heavens. 'O God, how sweet it is awaiting you. Almighty Lord, I am returning to you with a vast burden of errors. Accept me, and overlook my faults.'

Two voracious lions stormed into the arena and toppled him without a fight. Before long, half of his body was laid to rest in their stomachs.

Meanwhile, far away, the men shifted in their strange sleep, oblivious to the events unfolding outside the cave.

XVI

SNOW

The years marched on. Gallus passed away. The fleeting days reclaimed Archimedes' youth and, in turn, loaned it to his son Elias. Meanwhile, Archimedes nourished Elias' soul with the unadulterated teachings of Jesus until it was saturated with pure faith.

Outside the safety of their home, the Empire fell into crisis. Although attacks rained down from East and West, Domitian's legacy lived on. While the yoke still clung around their necks, Philadelphia's faithful soon realized that the situation in the western provinces was far worse.

The time had come to introduce Elias to harsh realities around them, and so, one day, Archimedes pulled Elias to his side and read him a report from Lyons. Despite his father's comforting presence, the letter scathed his young heart and left an indelible imprint on his innocent soul.

Marcus endured the torture with superhuman fortitude. He kept repeating, 'I am a Christian,' and they could extract no other answer from him. Their fury blazed, and they burned his flesh with red-hot iron blades. He stayed calm, though. His soul was free, and he was steadfast in his confession, as if that divine and exhilarating source that Jesus spoke of had given him strength.

They whipped him and beat him and locked him in with the beasts. Then they dragged his wounded body across the gravel and forced him onto a scalding iron chair. The putrid stench of scorching flesh filled the air. They wanted to quell his faith, but no words but the confession escaped his mouth. Finally, they decapitated him.

Then they tied Blandine to a column. She was a young slave in our congregation. None of the beasts would approach her, so they released her, whipped her, and put her in the scalding chair. When she still did not submit, they tied her in a net and threw the net to a bull. The bull rammed her with its horns and bucked her into the air. Her hope remained, and she continued to speak to Jesus.

They decapitated her too. As the people left, they said among themselves that no one in Gaul had ever tortured a woman like that before. We lost 18 of the faithful on that day.

Soon, Aurelius died and left the throne to his son Commodus – primarily because Commodus had made it clear that, were he not given the throne, he would take it himself. Unfortunately, Commodus lacked his father's morals. He was a coarse, savage, shallow, and cruel warrior who valued only physical strength. Like a slave, he dressed himself in lion skins and slew hapless gladiators in the amphitheatre while the palace watched on in dismay. One day, in a particular bout of enthusiasm, he took to the arena and crushed a hundred bears. Rome had fallen into the hands of a bloodthirsty madman, and it was painfully obvious what he would do to the Christians.

Popular mistrust towards the Christians had also intensified. Elias came to understand this one day on his way home from school when he overheard two street vendors talking.

'I've heard they esteem the lowest animal, the ass, and regard its utterances as holy.'

'Perhaps they learnt it from their prophet. They say his constant companion was an ass.'

'I bet the ass taught him what to say.'

They laughed boisterously.

'They don't worship like humans. They drink so much wine in their prayer ceremonies that they can't rise the next morning.'

'Do you know how they baptize new converts? They cover a baby in flour and put it in front of the convert and tell him to beat it. The wretched fool thinks he's beating dough and kills it with his blows. Then, they rip it apart, limb by limb, and lick its blood.'

'Ew! No wonder they're so secretive!'

'Certainly. They wouldn't be so secretive if they didn't have anything to hide. Why don't they have altars and temples like everyone else? None of the civilized

nations have ever even heard of their wretched god —
except the Jews, of course.'

'That miserable lot.'

'The Jews are a lot better off than these donkey-
worshippers. At least they have temples, sacrifices, and
ceremonies.'

In such an atmosphere, Elias passed into adulthood
and readied himself to continue his grandfather's work.
He learned to despise Commodus just as much as father
had despised Antonius until, one day, the market
buzzed with rumours that Commodus had been
murdered. It was hardly a surprise; his own relatives had
tried to do him in years before. Quickly, Elias stepped
out to investigate. The murder of an Emperor would
occupy the statesmen for some time and give the
Christians a chance to breathe.

Archimedes, now sixty-two, had also heard the news,
but he was unable to express any reaction. He was
bedridden, and his children sat anxiously around him..
They knew he did not have much time left. His
daughters' eyes filled with tears, and grief hung heavily
over the room.

Archimedes could hear his daughters weeping, but he
could not comfort them. He stared out the window.
Magnificent snowflakes were falling to the ground like
carriages conveying God's blessing. Everything was
covered in white. Archimedes watched them melt away.
As a child, he had excitedly examined the snowflakes
that fell only a few days a year. They were so orderly
and so beautiful, yet their lives were so short. Should the

annihilation of these gorgeous flakes be mourned? They rolled down the glass like teardrops, as if they were lamenting their own death. His lifetime had been as scant as the lifetime of these snowflakes.

What did it mean anymore? An hour, a year, or a thousand years – in the end, it was all the same. Joy or grief, hunger or satiation, intimacies or grudges – it all seemed but a fantasy. These feelings which had once overwhelmed his soul now fled in the face of death.

Archimedes gazed at the snow so long that the others also looked to see what was so fascinating. But could they see what he saw? Had he truly lived longer than the snowflakes? His age meant nothing anymore. Ah, whatever ends is truly short in duration, and whatever is short is small in value.

Archimedes felt someone take hold of his hands. Moving his gaze from the window, he focused his weak and bleary eyes on his son Fabius. Feebly, he asked, 'Has Elias not come?'

'No, father. But he will be here soon.'

After taking a few difficult breaths, Archimedes uttered, 'The Holy Book.'

Fabius rushed to the library and grabbed a Bible, hidden behind some voluminous histories. Archimedes held the Bible to his chest, weeping. Then, with all his might, he poured his thoughts into his children. 'It seems as if the world has never been. How ridiculous it is when people turn towards life, and how painful when they turn their back on it. When they should be wakeful, they are asleep; but when their time comes to sleep, they awaken.'

Elias appeared at the door. Softly, he approached his father's deathbed and took his hands. His father's eyes locked on his face.

'Father, it is true,' Elias reported. 'Commodus is dead.'

Archimedes no longer cared. This world did not involve him anymore. He was thinking of the life to come. He did not know what to expect. How would he meet God? What were the rituals of such a meeting? Whose help could he seek? How should he beg forgiveness? How could he stand before the magnificence of his Creator?

A thousand other questions filled him. At the same time, however, he savoured a newfound tranquillity. Now, he was truly going home. Simply sensing the state of being created erases all other matters. He felt as if he had been familiar with death his entire life but only now understood it. He felt as if he had been caged in this world and would now be freed.

This dual sensation put him into a strange rapture, and teardrops slid from his eyes. His tremulous expression silenced everyone. 'My children! I have a last request.'

They listened avidly.

'You will never see the world as I see it now until you reach my condition. But accept it from me: this world is not worth destroying yourselves for. All of you, by the grace of Jesus, have been guided. You know that even if you spent the nights weeping and the days praying, you could never sufficiently praise the process of coming into being from naught – let alone other blessings. Humankind does not tend to be grateful.'

Coughing cut short his last words, and Elias raised his head to stop the coughing. After heaving some deep breaths, Archimedes continued. 'Know that the blessing of coming into existence cannot compare to this blessing of guidance you have received. This blessing is beyond compare. God dispatched his most beloved being to invite his countless creatures to himself. Oh, what benevolence!'

Controlling his tears, he continued. 'Honour this blessing above other blessings. Know whatever bounty has been given to you is a means to prepare you for this greater bounty. Extend this blessing to others as well, for if they have no share in it, other blessings will bring them no joy. Without guidance and a clear goal, this world's bounties melt like flakes of snow.'

A bout of coughing again overwhelmed him. Although it soon subsided, it left him out of breath. Finally, with a voice more cracked than before, he continued. 'Your grandfather Iamelichos was determined to guide people on this path, and, determined, he died. Iamelichos...'

His words were left unsaid. Weeping, Elias dried his father's face with a handkerchief. Archimedes stared at the ceiling laboriously trying to breathe. He felt as if his arms and legs were no longer his. It was as if they never belonged to him. How easily, how effortlessly they were given to him; and how easily, how effortlessly they were taken away. His will was involved neither in receiving or returning them.

The girls began to sob loudly. Archimedes wanted to console them, but his tongue had also been taken back. He moved no more. Slowly, his ears also lost their ability, and the ceiling disappeared from above his head. He no longer gave or received anything from the world. Now he remained only himself, himself alone with himself. After a few moments, he also left the world, as if he had never been there.

As Archimedes passed on, Iamelichos and the other men shifted in their sleep, oblivious to the events unfolding outside the cave. Iamelichos had outlived his son.

XVII

THE FIRE

I n honour of his father, Elias commissioned a portrait
of him and hung it right next to the portrait of
Iamelichos. Looking at his face comforted him and
reminded him of the importance of their mission.

Once the agony of grieving had subsided, Elias
realized that the Empire had fallen into total chaos.
After regional armies had refused to accept the Senate's
choice of emperor, warlords had emerged all across the
land. In the anarchy, the Christians were suddenly
forgotten. There was no emperor to impose the laws —
or, when there was, he was too busy defending himself
against the soldiers. No one took the trouble to molest a
bunch of unarmed Christians.

After a few years, Septimius Severus prevailed. But
since he took power by force, he was bound to keep it
by force, and had little room to think about the
Christians. Constantly on the alert, he upheld his
personal philosophy: 'Make the soldiers free from want,

and do not bother about anything else.'

This policy – or, perhaps, lack of policy – freed the Christians to carefully continue their activities. As Domitian's laws gradually faded from popular memory, the Christian gatherings slowly emerged into the open. The missionaries' ardent words, spoken directly from the soul, awakened the slumbering masses, and the number of followers of Jesus of Nazareth grew day by day. Even after Severus' demise – which took eighteen years – the Christians remained relatively safe. Competition for the throne occupied the rulers' minds, so they did nothing to stem the rapid spread of the religion. The strict rules and severe punishments became a thing of the past.

Everywhere, houses of worship began popping up, until each area had its own bishop, including Philadelphia. However, despite their increasing numbers, Elias worried. Did the Christians see the truth as Jesus saw it? Did they worship the Creator as Jesus did? Were they as familiar with the truth as Jesus was? Did every fibre of their body tremble before God's majesty?

It alarmed him to see that the libertine Roman infidels – who used to make deals with their gods – no longer followed the rigid details of Jewish religious law when they converted. They still ate every meat and drank every impurity. Instead, the Christians had come to terms with Roman customs and had abolished the Law of Moses.

The followers of the Eastern religions no longer had to abandon their beliefs when they became Christians.

The trinity they believed in could now be found in Christianity. East and West, the pagans had been baffled by the Christians' unwillingness to depict God as a human. Now, that stumbling block had been removed. Those who had set their hearts on the beautiful and sad fable of a god being sacrificed for the sake of mankind had in fact worshipped Jesus all along. Now, anyone could become a Christian without changing much but a name.

Elias knew that not all the people of Philadelphia approved of the evolution of the faith. But what could he do? This chasm could not be closed by a few. He and his friends had to stand with the rest of the Christians. Perhaps one day there might be a respite, but, presently, it was time to fight the opponents of their religion.

So, in many ways and styles, Christianity was swiftly expanding. Now, Christians were found everywhere – in the troops, amongst the nobility, amongst the commoners, in the courts, in the marketplaces, amongst craftsmen, and amongst farmers. Every town now had at least one church. Now and then, there was still the occasional arrest, but, due to the grace of political instability, the Christians enjoyed relative peace.

Secure in the hope that his children would inherit a better future, Elias left the house to his son Matthias and surrendered his soul. Like his father, Matthias was a staunch believer, steadfast in the path of his elated ancestor Iamelichos. Nevertheless, he hesitated to oppose Philadelphia's church openly. Since they were still surrounded by idolaters, he felt obligated to stand by the faithful. But due to his differences of opinion, he did not get very involved with the church. Rather, he spent most of his free time reading.

Matthias was still not acquainted with the hardships of Christian life. For him, the tortures and mass killing he had heard of were just stories – stories like the epic of his ancestor Iamelichos. They now lived without fear of arrest, and only the old men and women remembered anything else.

And then, fate entrusted the orb of sovereignty to Decius. Decius put on the imperial robe at a time when anarchy had spread throughout the land. Armies were rising up and rebelling from every corner, and new emperors were ascending the bloodstained throne only to perish. Like them, Decius ascended a bloody throne – but, unlike them, he was determined to keep it. But how could he calm a land with a thousand monarchs?

His counsellors deemed it advisable to fortify the Roman religion. Let the people worship the Emperor as they had in the past. Let them acknowledge that Decius was under divine favour and regard themselves as his servants. No one would dare to revolt, and the era of Augustus and Hadrian would return. And so Decius drove forward the carriage of the Homeric religion, crushing the Christians beneath its evil wheels.

A terrible plague then spread its shadow over the entire land, and only death quietened its fearsome screams. In earlier times, the idolaters had blamed Christians for every flood, drought, and storm; now, spurred on by the temple priests, they did the same. The

Christians had invoked the wrath of the gods, and, in order to save themselves, they had to eradicate the Christians.

The gods, the people, and Decius had all united against the Christians. Retreating into his library, Matthias read tome after tome. Pulling out Iamelichos' old scrolls, he studied the lives of the ancient prophets while, from his portrait, Iamelichos stared down placidly at him. Sometimes, his servant Jassem read the scrolls to him. Together, they hid from the world until the day when his eldest son Zachariah came running in.

'Father!' Zachariah panted. 'The Emperor has issued a new decree. He's going to kill all the Christians who do not bow before the gods.'

The Hebraic script in front of Matthias became a blur.

'They're going to burn the big church tonight and turn the others into temples.'

'That's impossible,' Matthias objected.

'Father!' insisted Zachariah. 'Everyone's going to the church to get orders from the Bishop.'

Matthias looked down at the book. The letters rushed at him off the page as if they had suddenly come to life. He closed the book, dizzy.

Then, as if not by his own volition, he rose. His feet felt heavy, as if they were bearing the weight of his ancestors. 'Very well. Let's go.'

As they hastened towards the church, he noticed that several of the shops had closed, and many windows were shuttered. There were no children outside playing their usual games. *This can't be true*, he thought. *There are too many of us.* Off in the distance, a squadron of soldiers was marching to some ominous end. *In the olden days, the Christians were hidden. No one knew who they were. Nowdays, everyone knows who we are. We could all be arrested in hours.*

The Bishop was addressing a great crowd that had swelled outside the church. 'Brothers! Sisters! Seek patience through Jesus. Do not reciprocate violence with violence. God will compensate you for your pain. We are not the first Christians to suffer. Your ancestors have left you a glorious model. This church – '

Screams drowned out the Bishop's voice. Matthias looked back. Mounted soldiers were riding recklessly into the crowd, bearing torches. He watched helplessly as horsemen crushed a blockade of young men beneath their spears and blades. The horses bobbed up and down as they trampled the fallen, many of whom never even tasted the bite of steel. Relentlessly, more horsemen poured in from all sides, crushing the corpses as they closed in on the church.

The aged Bishop just stood there, gaping. Kicking him aside, the soldiers broke into the church. Inside, a cluster of women and children were clinging together. As the riders began smashing the innards, waves of men pushed their way towards the doors. The men fell, blocking the doors with a wall of bodies. The women and children began screaming, and the roars of the men mingled with the horses' neighs.

Another squadron drenched the church in oil before

hurling torches onto it. Flames leapt across the walls, and the soldiers inside forced their way out through the pile of bodies with their spears. Some of the bodies caught fire, and the screams intensified. Matthias and Jassem both rushed to the side door and fought their way into the smouldering church. Unable to distinguish the living from the dead, Matthias seized the first body he saw. Jassem came behind him with the corpse of a priest.

Timbers began falling as the crackling fire leapt across the wooden roof, and the soldiers backed away. Any minute, the building would fall.

But Jassem rushed back to the door.

'No!' Matthias yelled.

It was too late. Through the smoke, Matthias saw Jassem grasping the feet of an unmoving body – a woman, Matthias thought. The flames leapt up like a wall, and the church began to collapse. Before setting foot in any court, Jassem had burned in Jupiter's wrath.

Matthias stood staring at the door that Jassem had entered, never to return. Zachariah was tugging at him. 'Father! Run!' He didn't move. The stench of fire and flesh permeated the grounds.

Satisfied, the horsemen retreated from the church. They were not concerned with stragglers. They had a search operation to conduct, and the informants would be doing good business.

At home, Matthias and his family hastily took counsel. He commanded Zachariah, the eldest, to set off to the East. Hopefully, he would reach the Parthian lands – if he survived.

'Let me take Yuhanna,' pleaded Zachariah. Yuhanna was Zachariah's youngest brother. He had a special place in Matthias' heart.

Matthias shook his head. 'You are a man. You can handle yourself. But, should anything happen, he could never....' His voice dropped off, and he embraced Zachariah firmly. 'Go with God.'

'God be with you,' murmured Zachariah. Turning his face away, he disappeared out the door. His mother broke down crying.

Soon, the soldiers came for them, and they spent the night together in a cell. The guards said that most had surrendered, but the screams that pierced the cold night air suggested otherwise.

Just after daybreak, the temple tribunals went into session. The operation had been conducted with pure Roman efficiency. People informed on their neighbours; the soldiers arrested them; and the courts tried them. Swift and simple, the judges required neither witnesses nor proof. They only required the accused to bow before the temple gods. Although Decius wanted the accused to offer sacrifice, most were too poor to buy animals, so the court generously let them off on a guarantee.

Those who declined were given time to reconsider, and various torture implements eased their decision. Those who confessed to the religion of the state were promptly released with a certificate of impunity for the literate to read.

The Bishop was the first to be tried. As the sun had barely risen, lanterns still lit the temple turned courtroom. Yawning, the judge flipped through his ledger until he found a blank page. 'Let's make this short, Excellency the Bishop. Religion or life?'

'I am a Christian and will die a Christian.'

Stifling another yawn, the judge advised him, 'Do not be stubborn, Excellency. I do not want you to enter the arena on your own accord. Pity does not tread there.'

'I am not being stubborn, your Honour. Your soul is afflicted. You have sold yourself to this world – a place where no one profits. You should set your faith in Jesus and liberate your soul.'

Impatience flickered across the judge's face. 'You are mistaken if you think you can preach here. Forget yourself. Think of your unfortunate followers. Should you repent, many of them will too, and their blood will not be shed in vain.'

'They are far from unfortunate, your Honour. They are the happiest people I know.'

The alcoves were overflowing with the accused. 'Enough' snapped the judge, making a small scribble. 'You have one more day to reconsider. That is, if you survive the night.' The guards tugged on him, but the aged Bishop pushed them aside and shuffled along without support.

'Do not be selfish, Bishop,' the judge called after him. 'Think of the others.'

They put him in solitary confinement, and wardens

with hearts of stone attempted to break him down. Blood seeped from every part of his body, and large patches of his flesh were scorched. And yet he kept repeating the same infuriating phrase: 'I forgive you.'

Finally, they put him in the iron fist. Forcing his hands together, they shoved them into two half globes. Then, bit by bit, they turned the screw until his bones crushed.

Wincing, the Bishop closed his eyes. 'I...forgive...you.' Mercilessly, they continued, until, unexpectedly, the aged Bishop slumped down. As they examined him, an evil grin spread over their faces. The Bishop would no longer need another trial.

His groans had carried through the cells. 'Damnation to you!' Matthias yelled. 'May God not forgive you! What crime are you tormenting them for?' His voice was lost among the roars and whimpers. He could not think. Familiar voices kept crying out, driving away any clarity. Nevertheless, a plan to keep faith but evade torture revealed itself. Stealthily, he whispered it to his wife. She nodded. Then he whispered the plan to his daughter. She nodded too. He was about to tell Yuhanna, when, suddenly, the gate swung open.

Roughly, the guards seized him and his wife. Their daughter grabbed onto her, and she was pulled along with them. Frantically, his wife tried to grab Yuhanna, but the soldiers shoved him along with the other inmates. She began to scream, and the guards silenced her.

They were dragged into the Temple of Apollo. The

judge looked exhausted. Discreetly, Matthias approached him and murmured, 'Certificate of impunity against twenty golden coins.'

The judge glanced around furtively. 'I am glad you agreed to offer sacrifice and prostrate before the gods.' He signalled to a scribe. 'Write it up.' The scribe obeyed, and Matthias signed. 'You may pick up your certificates this afternoon.'

Matthias walked out of the courtroom a free man, his wife and daughter behind him. His wife was panicked, but he commanded her to go home. It was not safe out here. On foot, he went from temple to temple. He had to find Yuhanna.

Finally, he chanced across an old family friend selling confectionaries outside the Temple of Neptune. He had followed the soldiers inside when they had brought Yuhanna. With the foolhardiness of youth, Yuhanna had spat on the idols. They had taken him back to prison.

Matthias stood helplessly in front of the Temple. From the back of his mind, a voice reminded him he had to return to court to purchase his family's freedom. Sombrely, he did that, avoiding the gaze of his brethren awaiting trial. Then he went home and prayed.

Early the next morning, the soldiers emptied the jails. The remaining convicts were herded outside the city gates. There, servants of the state doused them with oil and set them ablaze. As soon as he heard, Matthias ran all the way across the city, but all he found were indiscriminate ashes. The pallor of death had set over the city.

Oblivious, the men in the cave rested peacefully in their sleep, occasionally shifting from side to side.

Decius did not last long, but his successor was even stricter, and the nine years of his rule were the darkest in Christian memory. *Sacrifice or be sacrificed*, the ignorant chanted, as the amphitheatres and thoroughfares became the graves of the faithful until – in true divine justice – the Emperor was skinned and hung by the Persian king.

Suddenly, the imperial successors had other priorities, and the Christians were returned to the loving hands of forgetfulness. As suddenly as it had started, the killing stopped. Ten years of torment had diminished but not depleted their ranks. The faithful had not yet been uprooted.

Gradually, the wounds were healed. The ruined church was refurbished and christened the Church of Bartholomew. One day, Zachariah's mother opened the door and found her son standing there. After wasting ten years wandering in small border towns, he had returned to carry on the mission. Tearfully, she told him about the loss of Yuhanna, and they mourned him anew.

Zachariah and Elias lent their full support to rebuilding the Christian cause. The Romans would never subdue them again. The Pope took the reins of the church, and, soon, troops and statesmen alike rinsed their mouths with the symbolic blood of Jesus. Christianity – or, at least, their interpretation of

Christianity – had become a roar which no one could ignore.

XVIII

THE WINDS OF CHANGE

The once glorious Empire was crumbling before their very eyes. Wearied by the continual infighting, not one but four emperors carved up the Empire between themselves. As before, Christianity resumed its spread until, in many provinces, it became the majority religion. Emboldened, the Christians erected a church across the street from the imperial palace, and openly Christian accountants began administering the royal payrolls.

Zachariah's son Yuhanna – named after his martyred uncle – now upheld his ancestors' tradition. Although many of his cousins had deviated from Iamelichos' strict monotheism, Yuhanna took his role as head of household seriously and always maintained Iamelichos' beliefs as well as his tale of epic courage.

In true divine irony, an Emperor named Diocletian

finally took one of the thrones. Like his namesake, he was a staunch idolater; but, unlike his namesake, he had no interest in further skirmishes with the Christians. Live and let live. However, while this Diocletian had no problem with Christian tax-collectors, he was less comfortable with Christian troops. The army was not a matter to be lax about. Finally, at the behest of some of his less charitable governors, he decreed the destruction of churches and holy books.

That night, soldiers came to Yuhanna's door and set fire to his library – kept intact for over two hundred years as a memorial to Iamelichos. Helplessly, Yuhanna watched as the priceless volumes burned to the ground. Although he managed to save his house, two of his sons fell in the continued legacy of bloodshed. He and his remaining son Marius sat in the half-burnt sitting room and stared up at the picture of Iamelichos for a very long time.

However, times had changed. It was impossible to overpower an enemy that viewed martyrdom as the highest attainment – especially when half the population sympathized with them. Christianity had also infiltrated the palaces, and rumours spread that one of the emperors had a Christian wife.

His son Constantine then took the throne. Not unsurprisingly, he avoided chasing after the Christians. And then, Yuhanna and the others listened in shock as the heralds announced the news that would forever change the world. After a divine vision, the Emperor Constantine had officially abolished the thousand-year-old religion of false gods. From now on, Rome would be a Christian empire.

Joy, incredulity, anger, hope, and excitement swept across the city. Many did not believe the news until the soldiers dismantled the temples, brick by brick. Jupiter's shamefully nude statue came down, and Cybele's revellers fell silent. It was hardly a loss; by now, few people actually believed in the gods, and it was a relief not to be surrounded by sacrificial carcasses anymore. Half the city was already Christian anyway. The selfless morals of the Christians attracted a lot more followers than the selfish manners of the pagans. The only people who were truly concerned were the idol carvers, who immediately switched over to hewing ornate crosses. But it was an abrupt change, and no one knew what to expect.

As the Christians held their heads high and the mischievous scuttled back into their shells, Yuhanna wished to God that Iamelichos could have witnessed the triumph of truth over falsehood. He wished he could have seen how the Christians were victorious with no army and no arms. He wished he could have seen how Hadrian's successor now bowed before God. He wanted to go to his resting place and tell him, but even he could not abide the terror of the cave.

Once, the people had bowed to the Emperor. Now, the Emperor bowed to the Pope. Initially, Yuhanna and the Christians celebrated; but soon, Yuhanna noticed a disturbing trend. Although he had relinquished his position as head of the Roman religion, Constantine was now exerting his influence on Christianity. As disputes over the divinity of Jesus peaked, Constantine appointed a council of bishops to ratify an official Christian creed.

I believe in one God, and in one Lord Jesus Christ, Son of God, the only-begotten, born of the Father before all ages. Yuhanna read and reread this simple assertion with concern. How many of his father's destroyed scrolls would have offered a different opinion. The officials had left him free to believe in Christianity – as long as it was their Christianity.

As Yuhanna diligently continued to keep the Saturday Sabbath, the neighbours began to whisper, for the religious council had pronounced Sunday the holy day. He could not help remembering his grandfather's stories about Attis' Sunday resurrection. He took his surviving son Marius out of school when the schoolmaster told him that Jesus had abolished the Law of Moses and only Jews abstained from pork.

The spread of the Christian ethos did give him hope. Every Sunday, the faithful who had once flocked to the Temple of Cybele now sat in the Church of Bartholomew and absorbed the ethical guidance of Jesus. Loving thy neighbour and caring for the poor became part of everyday discourse.

However, as the flocks increased day by day, Yuhanna became more concerned about Christian belief. Many of the converts seemed to be keeping their pagan beliefs under a Christian name. The Temple of Mithras had closed down, but its adherents still celebrated their winter solstice festival like clockwork – only now, on the pretext that it was the birthday of Jesus instead of the birthday of the sun. Instead of *light from light*, they now chanted *God from God*. Not to be outdone, Cybele's followers continued hauling pine trees down from the mountains – but now, to commemorate the nativity.

Yuhanna knew he wasn't alone. He, his son Marius, and even Theodosius, the local governor, still adhered to the divine monotheism. But they watched helplessly as the official Church dictated their belief and sentenced heretics to death.

Eventually, Yuhanna joined his forefathers. Marius was the only child he had left behind. Luminous and lucid, Marius did his best to uphold Iamelichos' tradition – but since he held no ecclesiastic position, the Church left him alone.

Thus employed, Marius reached ripe old age, confident that he was the eldest surviving member of Iamelichos' line. He often wished he could have met his fabled ancestor, and even once, had ventured into the eerie stillness of the cave. Of course, he had not been able to linger.

An avid audience for his stories, his friend Father Filus also wished he had lived in Iamelichos' time and could have asked him what the early Christians really believed. Religion had become so complicated. He differed with the Church but could not say so, for, as a priest, he was subject to the censure of the Council of Bishops. However, he was hardly silent. He still passed on his beliefs to the trustworthy, just as Iamelichos had done centuries before. Although he never spoke openly against the priesthood, he forbade wine and pork inside his own church. Rather than pronouncing religious edicts, he simply quoted Isaiah's words: *Woe to those who rise early to seek liquors and stay up late till wine mellows them. Woe to those in gatherings the lute, harp, tambourine, flute, and wine are found.* And of course, he quoted the renowned Iamelichos.

But although the idols had been shattered, they lived on in people's hearts. Constantine's official creed had led to more questions, not less. How could one God be multiple? Had God himself given birth? What exactly did it mean to be the Son of God? How did the crucifixion cleanse people of their sins?

It became popular to say these were 'unfathomable mysteries', and some of the Christians turned away. Were it not for Jesus' magnificent sermons and the inherent human inclination to worship God, their Christianity would have had little to offer.

Some of the former idolaters found it particularly difficult to wrap their minds around one issue: the Day of Resurrection. Was there life after death? Would the body be resurrected, or just the soul? If God was merciful, then why would he put people Hell? But if God was just, why wouldn't he put people in Hell? Surely, some people seemed to deserve it.

Day by day, the disputes grew more heated, until Theodosius – who had grown a long grey beard and now walked with a cane – feared that his people might forsake the religion. Thus, he arranged for a grand debate. At least, he could sway his own people.

The last religious debate in the palace – between Hadrian and the Christian rebels – had been left most unresolved. Now, unwittingly, they were about to resume it. Carefully, Theodosius prepared the palace for the occasion – but with considerably less excess than Diocletian had expended for the royal ball. But unlike Diocletian's private party, this debate was open to the masses – and they attended in droves.

Settled gracefully on his elegant throne, Theodosius supervised the proceedings. They had hand-picked a bishop, a priest, an idolater, and a sophist: namely, the Bishop of Philadelphia; Father Filus; an annoyingly outspoken ex-temple priest named Fahd; and a sophist with an unpronounceable Greek name. The city's finest judges sat next to Theodosius, ready to arbitrate. It was a historic event.

'Bring Arius in, lad,' Theodosius called to his page.

A spry man with bent fingers hurried in. 'Yes, Excellency?'

'Take note of these proceedings.'

Arius' face lit up. 'For the archives?'

'As you wish.'

Eagerly, Arius prepared his inkpot. He had long been promoted to palace librarian, and rightfully so, for he had studied every single text in the palace library and archives. Anything remotely historical fascinated him.

Theodosius looked out over the crowd from his throne – the throne once held by Diocletian. Marius stood out like a beacon among the crowd. Had Iamelichos sat in the same seat on that fateful night?

'Opening arguments,' Theodosius commanded.

The Bishop rose. 'Gentlemen! Do you believe the world has a Creator?'

Fahd took the challenge. 'Yes, but he does not interfere in this world. The divinities manage it. He has only created it – nothing more and nothing less.' None of them realized it, but almost the same words had been exchanged in the same palace three hundred years ago.

'But is the Creator wise or ignorant?'

'An ignorant being could not have created the world.'

'So did the Creator create aimlessly? Or did he have a goal for his creation?'

Fahd's sophist friend stepped in. 'We have no way of proving the Creator's intentions.'

'How strange,' replied the Bishop. 'Then this world is but a doomed and meaningless toy. How foolish and cruel it would be to create mankind, to instil in him love for life and the desire for perfection . . . only to leave him to annihilation. Tell me, what would you call a man who built a grand and precise apparatus, only to smash it to bits in an ill-omened, senseless, and silly game? Would he not be insane?'

How often had Iamelichos longed to say those words. But the sophist rejected them. 'We cannot know the Creator's aim. All we can know is what we see.'

'You claim that God will raise the dead,' added Fahd. 'But no one has ever seen the dead return to life. And how could the dead return to life after their bones had decayed? It is absolutely impossible.'

'God has brought some of the dead to life through our master Jesus, and history has recorded this,' replied the Bishop. His voice reflected the calm certainty of faith.

'Perhaps history has made an error,' Fahd objected curtly. 'This has no basis.' Arius frowned.

'It does not need to be the basis of anything,' replied the Bishop. 'When the Day of Resurrection comes, the world will undergo fundamental changes. It will not operate according to the same rules it does now. Although the dead do not rise now, we have no reason to think they will not rise then.' He paused to let his point sink in. 'Second, nothing is beyond the power of God. If the Creator was powerful enough to create the world, he is powerful enough to raise us from the dead.'

'We cannot accept this.'

'Why?' asked Filus. Attention shifted to him. 'We can understand the Creation. Why not the Resurrection? Why limit ourselves to what we see and hear now?'

'Prove it,' demanded Fahd.

'The prophets have prophesized it,' Filus reminded him.

Fahd looked unconvinced.

'And our inherent moral perception confirms it,' continued Filus. 'Creating mankind without a Day of Resurrection would be futile. A wise Creator would not err so. Why bear all the pain and suffering of this rough and colourless existence only to pass into annihilation?'

Arius lifted his pen for a moment. 'Thousands of pious and ascetic individuals have affirmed its existence,' he called out. 'Truth is chaste; it only unveils itself to the worthy.'

Theodosius shot him a stern look, and he returned to scribing. The discussion continued well into the night. Eventually, the panel disbanded, but with no resolution. It was to be expected: the debate was really to satisfy the audience, not the debaters.

As he was leaving, a particularly prominent judge by the name of Judge Stevens passed by Arius. 'I have to go,' he whispered. 'Come to the courtroom tomorrow and tell me what happens.'

Gradually, the crowd thinned, until only a handful of Christian adherents remained. Theodosius looked wearier than usual. 'Words alone cannot resolve this question. We need proof. How can we convince them to believe in something they cannot see?'

'Excellency,' reassured Filus, 'they can see it. We do not just see with our eyes and ears. We see with our intellects too. They are not doubting because of their intellects. They are doubting because of their desires. Their human instincts are blurred, for they are attached to this world.'

'True,' agreed Theodosius, 'but we still need to assuage their doubts.'

'The Father is right,' concurred the Bishop. 'Human beings have always tried to evade responsibility. They will follow anyone who tells them there is no Resurrection, even if that person's words are devoid of reason.'

Theodosius raised his hands to the sky. 'O God, why do you not show a sign? Why leave your servants in ignorance?'

Filus stared at him with some concern. He had never heard Theodosius speak like this before. 'Do not say such things, Excellency,' he advised. 'God has already given us enough signs. He has given us the prophets and our intellect. His wisdom is above all wisdom, and his love is above all love. After all this, should he send more signs? Those who intend to turn away will do so no matter how many signs he shows.'

Theodosius pressed his hands to his temples. 'I am tired. Let me rest.'

Upon his exit, the stragglers dispersed. Despite the late hour, Filus headed directly for his church. The streets were silent. Pushing the heavy wooden door open, he found the church unsurprisingly deserted. After lighting a single candle, he kneeled before the altar.

'O God,' he prayed, 'I fear that Theodosius may begin to doubt. What will happen to your servants here if he does? You are aware of what transpired here in earlier times.'

A couple tears flowed from his eyes as he recalled the tragic tales of his former brethren. 'God, your wisdom is above all wisdom, and we have faith in your plan.' He took a deep breath. 'Still, I must ask something of you, if you deem it wise.'

A strange feeling overcame him. Although he had spent many nights in here before, he felt as if the church itself seemed to be listening. A shiver ran down his spine, and, with all his heart, he made his final request. 'Bring us a sign. Show your power to these people. Bring them a sign that none can overlook. Convince them once and for all.'

PART THREE

XIX

THE AWAKENING

Iamelichos moved slightly. The midday sun cast a faint light into the cave. Looking up, he saw the stony, uneven ceiling in place of the sky. *What a sleep*, he thought, disoriented. He could not quite recall where he was or why he was here.

Soon, the confusion passed. With a start, he remembered the dreadful events of the night before – the feast, the flight through the desert, and the retreat to the cave. More certain of his bearings, he tried to get up. Severe pain shot through his back. Chiding himself on his softness, he resolved to spend more time sleeping on the bare earth. After forcing himself up, he waited for the pain to subside before calling out, 'Maximilian! Joannes! Friends!'

Immediately, Antonios started up and then snapped back down, as if his back were nailed to the rock. Sheepishly, he hauled himself up to his elbow and shook Dionysios, who was sleeping next to him. 'Brother!

Wake up! We've slept for a long time.'

'Hadrian,' murmured Dionysios. 'Diocletian...the palace....' Blinking a few times, he too tried to sit up, only to sink back down to the stone again.

One by one, the others came to their senses. As if by unspoken agreement, they sat silently while the giddiness of sleep wore off their bodies and souls.

Rubbing his back, Antonios limped over to the mouth of the cave and checked on Comteri, who was still soundly asleep on the rock. Martinos and Exakoustodianos followed him. Closing their eyes to slits to avoid the dim mountain sun's stinging rays, they retreated back into the comfortable darkness of the cave.

'How long have we been sleeping?' asked Antonios.

Martinos glanced outside. 'No more than a few hours. We went to sleep a little before noon, and now it is only a little past noon.' He paused doubtfully, massaging his sore arms. 'But I do feel as if I have slept a lot. Perhaps we slept for a whole day and didn't realize it.' His stomach growled, and he clapped his hand over it, embarrassed.

'It is not improbable,' agreed Exakoustodianos. 'We were quite exhausted.'

'I am absolutely ravenous,' added Dionysios. 'If we had slept only two or three hours, we wouldn't be this hungry – especially since we ate before going to sleep.' He looked at them quizzically. 'Are you as hungry as I am?'

One by one, they nodded in agreement. But Iamelichos could not shake a strange sensation that there was something more to their sleep. Confused, he glanced at Maximilian and Joannes. They were looking at him with the same bewildered expressions.

'Your God knows how long you have slept,' declared Maximilian. 'There is no point in discussing it. We had better think about how we will get our hands on some food. I have never experienced the like of this hunger. I do not think it is simply due to not eating for a couple days.'

'We should have brought along provisions,' commented Exakoustodianos. 'Leaving now will be extremely dangerous.'

'Strange,' mused Antonios. 'I have often gone without food, but I have never suffered as I am now. I feel as if I am dying of starvation.'

'My innards feel like they are tearing apart,' agreed Dionysios.

Maximilian searched his ceremonial robes in vain. 'Who has money? '

They all examined their clothing hopefully, searching for a forgotten pocket or purse. Unfortunately, their formal attire had not been designed for practicality.

Antonios' eyes sparkled. 'Wait!' he cried. Triumphantly, he extracted a not-so-valuable coin from the bottom of his pocket. Their faces lit up. 'I don't know why I put this here. I never carry coins with me.'

'It is the grace of God,' Iamelichos replied. 'He is benevolent towards his servants and has provision for us. Even just one portion of food will suffice us for a couple days. One of us needs to procure some pure food from the city. Our hunger is not normal.'

'Why the city?' asked Martinos. 'I'll go to Raqim.'

He was already halfway out the cave when Maximilian stopped him. 'Hold on! We do not know how long we have been here, or what is happening down there. Should news of our escape have reached Raqim, we cannot return. They would recognize us at once.'

Deflated, Martinos stepped back.

'We must go to the city,' Maximilian instructed. 'Also ... we do not know who sells pure food around here.'

'No one sells any,' murmured Antonios.

'Then I will go to the city,' vowed Iamelichos. 'I know this area best.'

'Be careful,' Joannes advised him. 'Avoid confrontation at all costs. Be extra polite to the pagans and the tradesmen, lest they discover our hiding place. Should they follow you, we will all be stoned to death — unless we give up our religion. And, in that case, we would be deprived of deliverance and salvation.'

Iamelichos smiled and tidied up his robes 'The task may be dangerous, but there is no other way.'

Martinos looked at him with wide eyes. 'Please return quickly, Excellency Iamelichos, or else we will get worried.'

'I'll try to return before dark,' promised Iamelichos, 'although, most likely, I'll have to spend the night in the city. If I do not return, you can assume I was caught. But, I assure you, no matter what happens, I will never divulge your whereabouts.'

'May nothing untoward happen to you, Excellency Iamelichos!' invoked Antonios.

After glancing at the sleeping dog, Iamelichos set off down the slopes. He thought he remembered more greenery; the slopes seemed dustier and steeper than they had been before. He could not find their path. It was as if all traces of their presence had been erased. Could God have hidden their tracks?

Eventually, he found his way down to the road. Still half-asleep, he started heading north, not thinking of the danger. He walked for some time without meeting anyone until, suddenly, a rider in full military uniform came galloping towards him at full speed.

How could I have been so careless? he chided himself, wrapping his scarf around his face. He looked around. There was nowhere to hide on the open road. Succumbing to destiny, he planted himself firmly on the ground and lowered his face.

In a cloud of dust, the rider passed him by. Astonished, Iamelichos stood fixed in place. Could some crisis have come over Philadelphia great enough to distract attention from them? He glanced back. The rider was wearing a brass Roman helmet, an embroidered blue cloak, and grey Gallic trousers! Diocletian would have had a fit if he had seen any of his soldiers dressed like that. Was he an ambassadorial guard?

The sun glinted off his pike-like weapon and gargantuan shield, engraved with an ornate lion. It was breathtaking. Craning his neck, the rider looked back too, and they locked eyes momentarily before the rider spurred his horse on.

Your God will shower upon you his mercy. As before, the words came to Iamelichos' mind unbidden. His morale uplifted, Iamelichos calmly continued on his way towards Philadelphia, only veering off the main road once he could see the cemetery and olive groves. Hopefully, the soldiers had not yet discovered the secret passage.

Abruptly, however, he stopped dead in his tracks. There was something wrong with the gates. Where were the gods? Had the effigies fallen down? Had God finally smashed Janus in his wrath? Curiosity overwhelming caution, Iamelichos edged closer. The gates were the wrong colour. *Am I in the wrong city?* he wondered.

An oddly dressed man – presumably, a guard – approached him, and he hastened through as inconspicuously as he could. Behind him, the guards were whispering in a strange accent, something about a Persian ambassador. He couldn't quite make out their dialect – Alexandrian, perhaps?

Maybe they put in new gates, Iamelichos theorized. Maybe Hadrian was displeased with old ones. Maybe they didn't have time to put the statue of Janus back up. He couldn't think of any other explanation. But the uniforms. Did Hadrian forbid those too?

Remembering his duty, he grudgingly traipsed up to the Temple of Janus. Better an obsequy now than to risk losing his cover. But, suddenly, his mouth dropped. Where was the Temple of Janus? Had there been an earthquake?

Keeping his head down, he disappeared back into the streets, oblivious to the fact that the guards were still pointing and staring at him. *What strange clothes*, he thought, glancing left and right. He wracked his brain and tried to recall if he had forgotten some heathen festival. Or had he spent so much time in the palace that he had lost touch with the common man?

Maybe I'm dreaming, he thought. This seemed like the most logical explanation. He did still feel as if he were half-asleep. Pressing his lids together, he willed himself to awareness, then opened his eyes again. The same strange people milled around him.

The food, he thought. Let me just get the food.

An impromptu market seemed to have overtaken the Philadelphian streets. Farmers and fruit-sellers were hawking their wares – but in a most peculiar manner. 'Six sesterces a dozen! A *dinar* a pound!'

What were they talking about? Were they all foreigners? Had Philadelphia had a sudden influx of refugees?

Iamelichos could take it no more. Masking his astonishment, he stopped an olive-skinned man. 'Excuse me, sir. Could you tell me the name of this town?'

The man looked Iamelichos up and down. 'Philadelphia, wayfarer, this is Philadelphia.'

A clamour burst out in front of him. Iamelichos looked up. One of the stallholders had seized a man by the collar. Hastily, he edged away as a crowd began to gather.

All of a sudden, the man's raspy voice rose above the din, clear as a bell. 'I swear by the ghost of Paul that I've paid.'

Iamelichos wheeled around.

The merchant let go. 'I swear by the Holy Mother you did not.' He started to empty his pockets to the crowd. 'Look, this is all I have. It's not half of what you owe.'

'Perhaps you dropped it.'

'Swear by Jesus the son of Mary that you paid.'

'I did, I swear I did.'

Could they all be Christians? Was this why they felt so comfortable to take Christian oaths under the penalty of death? He was dying to ask, but, even if he hadn't been trying to avoid unnecessary arguments, he was tongue tied.

Swiftly, he walked on towards the end of the road, only to meet a greater surprise. *The Church of Bartholomew.* Could he be reading that right?

Mouthing the inscription, he glanced up. A magnificent cross had been erected atop the building's spire. His eyes bulged. Climbing the steps, he peered in. An evocative statue of an emaciated man nailed to a cross was affixed to the wall. Judah's lifeless face flashed through his mind, and, although he had never seen such an icon before, he knew it must be Jesus.

Inside, a few people were seated on broad wooden benches and appeared to be engaged in prayers. He wanted to speak to them ... but what to ask? He could not believe his eyes.

Perhaps this was all part of some grand intrigue. He would not put anything past Diocletian. Rushing back down the street, he recognized some familiar depictions of Apollo and Mithras in the shops. Strangely, he found them reassuring.

He was not sure why, but he was relieved to find that the bakery still stood. Of course, the exterior had completely changed, but the archetypical scents of wheat and yeast comforted him. Like a man lost in a vast desert, he took refuge from the madness in the tiny shop, only to lay eyes on the baker.

O my God! he thought helplessly. Why are they all dressed so strangely?

The baker stared back. 'Aye?' he asked.

Aye? Iamelichos wondered. 'Ten loaves please.'

Without taking his eyes off Iamelichos, the baker gathered up ten loaves with his grungy hands while Iamelichos handed over the coin, hoping it would be enough. It wasn't worth very much. As the baker took the coin, Iamelichos arranged the loaves securely in his kerchief, relieved that the baker wasn't asking for more.

The baker stared down at the coin, then up at Iamelichos, then down at the coin again. Finally, he disappeared into the back, and Iamelichos assumed he went to get change.

A voice drifted out. 'It's inscribed with the Emperor Hadrian.'

'We're in luck,' the baker said, emerging with a heavy-set, churlish assistant, caked in flour.

The assistant stared down Iamelichos. 'So, how many

of these have you found?'

'What?' asked Iamelichos.

'Don't think we don't know your secret,' the baker chimed in.

Iamelichos was sure they hadn't recognized him. 'Sir?'

'Look friend,' warned the assistant, blowing his foul breath on Iamelichos, 'I don't know where you come from, but don't think of trying to trick us. We can outsmart seven Satans.'

'I don't know what you are talking about,' Iamelichos told him.

The baker held out the coin victoriously. 'Then where did you find this treasure?'

Whatever what was going on seemed to be taking a turn for the worse. 'I don't know what you mean by treasure,' he said in carefully measured tones, 'but you can keep the change.' Perplexed, he took the bread and headed out.

Like lighting, the muscular assistant seized his arm. 'Not so fast.'

'Look, friend,' the baker proposed, 'let's talk fair. Don't be greedy. You know what will happen if we inform the officials. First, you will be penalised for not reporting it, and, second, you'll have to pay heavy taxes. You won't have much left. So be wise. We'll take half the taxes and show you how to get rid of the rest.'

'You are insane, sir,' Iamelichos advised him.

'This one seems really greedy.'

'We have no choice but to hand him over.'

Angrily, Iamelichos wrested his arm free and ran from the shop. As the bakers ran after him, a crowd formed.

'He found treasure and won't pay taxes!' yelled the baker's assistant. 'As if this country doesn't have any laws!'

Iamelichos was mobbed by complete strangers. He couldn't see a single friend or relative even though he had lived in Philadelphia his entire life. No one seemed to recognize him either. Could this be real? Why didn't he understand anything anymore? Why were they acting like this?

Cutting through the crowd, more soldiers in blue cloaks apprehended him. Flooded with disappointment and sorrow, Iamelichos hung his head. He had failed.

XX

THE COIN

'Loan sharks,' grumbled Judge Stephens as the last debtor of the day disappeared out the door. 'I don't know what Philadelphia is coming to.'

Sighing, he turned to Arius. 'How did it go last night?'

'Not good, your Honour,' answered Arius dismally. 'Theodosius... I'm worried he might be siding with the sophists.'

The judge furrowed his brow in concern. 'This is disturbing news. Even worse than last year's tax scandal. You – of all people – recall what Philadelphia was like before Christian rule. I'd hate to return to those days.'

'The central government would never allow it,' promised Arius brightly. But he lowered his head.

'The central government can't do anything but collect tithes.'

Suddenly, the court porter burst in. 'Your Honour! The Via Porta baker has turned in a treasure hoarder!'

The judge raised his eyebrows.

Undaunted, the podgy porter displayed a frayed leather pouch. 'Your Honour, he found an old-time coin and tried to buy bread with it!'

'Buying bread with his treasure-coin, eh?' chided the judge. 'Why, that riff-raff deserves a good wrist-slapping. Sorry, the court's closed for today.'

'Your Honour,' intervened Arius, 'perhaps we had ought to take a look at it.'

'The coin or the criminal?' muttered the judge. Arius flushed – but only mildly. 'Very well. Bring him in.'

'I have a better idea,' suggested the judge as the porter rushed out. 'Let's put all the Via Porta merchants on trial tomorrow instead.'

'Excellent idea, your Honour,' replied Arius, only half-listening; he was waiting for the coin.

The guards opened the door. 'This way, Excellency.' The judge cocked his ears. Excellency?

A strange man stepped into the courtroom. He carried himself with the grace of a nobleman, and yet his eyes reflected the humility of a saint. Elaborate, embroidered robes fluttered around him. Unhesitatingly, his eyes locked onto the courtroom cross, and he stared intently, seemingly oblivious to the proceedings. The judge decided then and there that – wherever he was from – a man of such peace and dignity could have done no wrong.

Triumphantly, the porter emptied the pouch onto the judge's bench. Out rolled a grungy coin, crumbling around the edges. Brushing off the dirt, the judge held it up and squinted.

'Hadrian,' whispered Arius excitedly. 'From the dynasty of Antonius.'

The stranger's eyes were still fixated on the cross. 'You tried to buy bread with this?' the judge demanded in disbelief.

'Your Honour...' voiced the defendant. His gaze wandered back up to the cross. 'Are you a Christian?'

The judge nudged Arius. 'Is he talking Latin?'

'He is,' Arius whispered, 'but I've never heard that dialect before.'

The judge raised his voice. 'Where did you get this coin?' The man stared blankly back. 'The coin... where did you get the coin?'

'Your Honour,' Iamelichos replied haltingly, 'my friend gave it to me. I do not understand what is so unusual about it. I do not understand any of this.' He hesitated. 'Your Honour... are you a Christian?'

The judge surveyed him quizzically. 'Of course I'm a Christian. Actually, I was baptised as a child – even before the Emperor.'

Iamelichos grasped at a bench for support. 'Your Honour... have the Emperor Hadrian and His Excellency Diocletian become Christians?'

'Is he mad?' the judge whispered to Arius.

'He doesn't look mad,' Arius whispered back.

'No, he doesn't,' agreed the judge. He cleared his throat. 'Sir, I regret to inform you that the Emperor Hadrian no longer walks the earth.'

'He has died,' whispered Iamelichos. 'Thank God.'

The judge studied him for a couple moments. 'Where are you from, sir?'

'Philadelphia.'

'Philadelphia!' interrupted Arius. 'This Philadelphia?'

Iamelichos' eyes flickered around the courtroom. He examined the guards, the judge, the walls, and the benches — but, most of all, the cross. 'I am from Philadelphia,' he affirmed. 'But... maybe not this Philadelphia. I am from the Philadelphia the Emperor Hadrian was in yesterday, before he... before he... died.'

'I have visited that Philadelphia too,' confided Arius, 'but only in the palace scrolls.' He approached Iamelichos. 'Do you know the year?'

'It is... DCCCXL. Yes, that's it. DCCCXL.'

Arius figured carefully. 'DCCCXL... correct. Hadrian's last years. Almost a century and half after the birth of Christ.' His eyes suddenly glittered with excitement. 'Judge Stephens! In that era, a brute named Diocletian governed Philadelphia!'

'Amazing,' commented the judge. 'He should replace the palace history tutor.'

'Your Honour,' voiced Iamelichos. 'I should like to know. When did the Emperor Hadrian... er... die?' His brown eyes were wide with the sincere desire to know.

'Three centuries ago,' Arius softly told him.

'Three centuries!'

'Yes.' Arius calculated on his fingers. 'Three centuries since the most untimely death of Hadrian.

Four hundred and thirty-seven years since the birth of Christ. MCXL years since the founding of Rome – '

'Impossible,' objected Iamelichos.

'Why do you say that?' asked Arius.

'My friends and I left this accursed place yesterday. Hadrian was here. I saw him.'

'Sir, the Emperor Hadrian – ' reminded the judge.

Arius shot him an intent glance, and the judge fell silent. 'Why did you leave?' asked Arius.

'Because they wanted to kill us.'

'Why?'

'Because we refused to bow before the Emperor.'

'You mean the Emperor Hadrian.'

'Yes.'

'Why did you refuse to bow before the Emperor Hadrian?'

'Because we do not bow to anyone but God.'

Arius scrutinized him like a history book. His story, his clothes, his accent, his personality... they all matched. 'Who are you?'

'I am no stranger to this town.'

'Your name,' insisted Arius. 'What is your name?'

Iamelichos towered over Arius, and Arius edged the slightest step back. 'Iamelichos.'

Arius drew in his breath. 'Which Iamelichos?'

'Iamelichos, counsellor to Diocletian, the governor of Philadelphia.'

Arius' jaw dropped. The judge dropped his pen, and the guards backed away.

'Iamelichos the corpse?' whispered the judge.

Iamelichos was utterly speechless.

'The story on the silver tablet,' murmured Arius. 'How many of you are there?'

'Seven.'

'In the cave on Mount Angelos?'

Iamelichos looked at him suspiciously. 'How do you know?'

'Did you... did you...' Arius could not quite get the words out. 'Did you just come from the cave?'

'Yes,' replied Iamelichos patiently, 'and now my friends are waiting for me to bring back bread. They are very hungry.'

'I imagine,' murmured Arius. 'But... what have you been doing all this time?'

'Sleeping.'

'Sleeping?'

'All night, we ran through the wilderness. When morning came, we climbed Mount Angelos. We had not slept since early the day before. So we took some rest. We have only been awake a few hours.'

Arius could not believe what was happening. Experimentally, he reached out and touched Iamelichos' shoulder. It was real. 'Do you have a house in Philadelphia?'

'Yes.'

'Where?'

'Poseidon Avenue.'

'We have no Poseidon Avenue,' interrupted the judge.

'True,' admitted Arius, 'but the streets used to have

pagan names.'

The judge considered it. 'Now that I think about it, I do remember a Poseidon Avenue. I had an uncle who lived off there, by the old temple.'

Arius clasped his hands together excitedly. 'Could you take us to your house?'

An unmistakeable – and, to Arius, exquisitely beautiful – yearning crossed Iamelichos' antiquated face. 'Certainly.'

The treasure forgotten, the three of them clambered into Arius' carriage. With increasing confidence, Iamelichos directed them through the streets. On one side loomed the Coliseum; and, on the other, the Church. Soon, they disappeared into alleyways as ancient as Philadelphia itself. Old women in black shawls carried baskets on their heads, and bare-footed children darted through the streets. It began to feel more like home.

The carriage ground to a halt in front of a modest antique villa. Eagerly, Iamelichos sprung out. He was finally returning to hearth and home. Gallus would take the reins at the door, and Maria would be waiting worriedly inside. At his voice, Archimedes would come barrelling down the stairs, and Iamelichos would surprise him with the sweets hidden inside his pockets. He felt the sides of his robes. Where were his pockets?

A wrinkled old servant maid opened the door and crossed herself. Then she shut the door and shattered his illusions.

Arius knocked again. The door opened a smidgen.

'Whose home is this?' he inquired.

Keeping one eye on Iamelichos, the old woman replied, 'This is the residency of Excellency Marius. What is your business?'

'Judge Stephens has come to speak with Excellency Marius.'

The servant's slippers clacked along the tile with a speed unusual for her age. 'Holy Mary,' she was muttering. 'It's like the walking dead.'

Iamelichos wondered if she was talking about him.

Soon, she returned, slightly more composed. 'Please, come in.'

They filed into the courtyard. Iamelichos took a good look around. It was his courtyard… and yet it wasn't. The fountain that he had built with his own hands was still flowing. But now, its mossy tiles were crowned with a statue of a bashful lady, veiling her face as she cradled her child, swathed in cloth. It was beautiful. He would have put it there himself.

Tripping over an unexpected row of bricks, Iamelichos stepped into his home. An old man was waiting authoritatively by the door. It was not Gallus.

'Welcome, gentlemen. Please, come in,' the old man said. Suddenly, he caught sight of Iamelichos. The two locked eyes for a moment before Iamelichos averted his gaze and resigned himself to being led to his sitting room.

Judge Stephens and Arius were already seated, but neither of them noticed Iamelichos enter. They were too busy staring up at the wall as intently as Iamelichos had been staring at the courtroom cross. Iamelichos looked up to see what they were staring at.

It was him – and a very flattering portrait of him as well.

An awkward silence filled the room. The servant woman returned and hastily handed out glasses of barberry juice.

Finally, Iamelichos spoke up. 'Excellency Marius, is this your house?'

'Yes…. Excellency.' In the confusion, they had neglected introductions.

'Who did you buy it from?'

'I did not buy it. I inherited it from my forefathers.' He indicated the portrait. 'All the way back to our great forebear Iamelichos, may God have mercy upon his soul.'

Iamelichos did not know what to say.

The judge pointed to the portrait. 'Is that Iamelichos?'

'It certainly is,' said Marius. 'Gave our maid quite a scare too, when she saw your guest. I had to remind her that Iamelichos was martyred during the reign of Hadrian and has not been reported to have walked from the dead since.'

The judge paled.

'O God,' implored Iamelichos. 'Could this be true?'

Arius was thinking the unthinkable. He opened his mouth, then closed it, then opened it again. Finally, he voiced, 'Have you heard of the Prophet Ezra?'

Marius smiled a bittersweet smile. 'My great-grandfather had acquired a rare scroll about him ... before it was burned during Diocletian's reign.'

Iamelichos looked alarmed. 'Not that Diocletian,' Arius whispered to him.

'The Prophet Ezra wanted to see how God revived the dead,' continued Marius, 'so God killed him and returned him to life after a hundred years.'

Closing his eyes, Iamelichos placed his hands on his brow. This is what we prayed for right before we went to sleep. Why doesn't God make truth victorious? Why doesn't he bring a great sign that will end all doubt?'

Arius grinned at Iamelichos. 'You, Excellency, are like three Ezras! You have slept for three hundred years. Excellency Iamelichos, how I long to know the purpose of that sleep.'

Marius spluttered, spilling barberry juice across the elegant divan. 'Excellency Iamelichos? From the cave?'

'All these years, we thought they were dead,' Arius told him. 'But they were really asleep. Very, very, very sound asleep.'

Marius clasped his chest and took a few deep breaths. 'The legends – they do say this. They said the men of the cave were alive... and staring at them.'

'You mean, asleep and staring at them,' corrected Arius. 'Ever since I read the silver tablet, I have always wondered about this. How could seven corpses inspire such fear into the hearts of brave men? One of Hadrian's commanders wrote a memoir about it. His name was... Sanctus, I think. His book is in the library. He swore up and down that they were alive, but so awesome that none could approach them. He always blamed himself for burying them alive. It is too bad he never lived to this day. Extraordinary!'

Iamelichos looked up at Marius. 'Archimedes?' he whispered.

Marius rose from his chair and kneeled at Iamelichos' side. Tremulously, he kissed Iamelichos' hand. 'Excellency Iamelichos, I am your descendant from Archimedes' line.'

'Archimedes' line!'

'Archimedes was my great-great grandfather.' Marius pointed up to a smaller portrait. 'That was him.'

Iamelichos filled his eyes with the portrait the way a thirsty man would fill himself with drink. How handsome Archimedes had become! How dignified! How noble!

Suddenly, a sadness crossed him. Archimedes was gone, really gone. Maria was gone. Gallus was gone. Everyone and everything he had ever known was gone — and in its place was something very good, but something utterly foreign to him.

Iamelichos embraced his grandson, and the two of them wept. No one interrupted them. Finally, Iamelichos wiped away his tears and looked afresh at the room. 'What year did you say it is?'

'MCXC years after the founding of Rome,' calculated Arius, 'or Four hundred and thirty-seven years after the birth of Christ.'

'Three hundred years,' murmured Iamelichos.

'Many generations,' added Marius. 'More than fifty

emperors. Much suffering.'

Iamelichos took a deep breath. 'Is that over now?'

Marius nodded. As the two of them caught up, Marius called for the servant woman, who reappeared carrying a tray of warm bread, green olives, red grapes, and farmer's cheese. She set it down in front of Iamelichos while keeping herself as far from him as humanly possible. Meanwhile, the judge and Arius were conferring between themselves.

'Please, Excellency,' invited Marius.

Iamelichos looked down at the food. 'My friends are waiting for me to bring food,' he said softly. 'It would not be proper for me to eat before them.

'You haven't eaten in three hundred years!' Arius told him. 'We will bring them food soon. Right now, you need to strengthen yourself. We don't want you to face the governor on an empty stomach.'

Iamelichos sat up alertly. 'The governor?'

'Events are unfolding that are not unconnected with your awakening,' Arius told him. 'You must see the governor before you return to the cave.'

'It will only take a short while,' promised the judge.

'Don't worry, you won't have to flee this time,' Arius assured him. 'You are our guest.'

Hesitantly, Iamelichos took a small bite. Despite his ravenous hunger, his insides rebelled. He chewed laboriously and then swallowed. The food felt like fire. Eventually, he managed to consume a small piece of the loaf and a cup of water.

Soon, they made for the palace. Iamelichos was not

sure what a Christian palace was supposed to look like, but, as it happened, it looked just like the palace of Diocletian.

He glanced over at Marius. Had Marius fallen into the palace intrigues just as he had? Or had his grandchildren eschewed politics?

A man who was just as white-bearded as Marius was settled on Diocletian's throne. 'He's not just a Christian,' Arius whispered to him. 'He's a true follower of Jesus.'

Iamelichos looked back at him, perplexed. Could a true follower of Jesus live in a palace like this?

Theodosius' eyes lingered upon Iamelichos. 'Hail, friends. What brings you here at this late hour?'

Arius stepped forward. 'Your Excellency, the sleepers have arisen.'

Theodosius stared at him incomprehensively. 'What?'

'The martyrs have returned from the cave.'

Theodosius' face reddened. 'I am in no mood for jest. If this is about the debate —'

'It is not,' affirmed Marius. He spoke with the same gravity as Iamelichos. 'Our forefathers have awakened.'

Theodosius' eyes widened in fear and disbelief.

As Arius enthusiastically narrated the tale, Theodosius rose from his throne and paced back and forth. Iamelichos knew that it was not Diocletian, and yet all he could see was Diocletian, preparing a new onslaught against the Christians.

Finally, Theodosius settled back down. 'This

requires proof. I cannot simply accept it.'

Arius' face fell.

'What about the tablet?' asked the judge.

Arius brightened again. 'With your permission, I would bring the record from the royal archives.' Theodosius nodded, and Arius rushed from the room. Like lightning, he returned, brandishing a thick silver tablet. He handed it over to Theodosius.

Theodosius studied it. 'Excellency...Iamelichos?' Iamelichos nodded. 'Can you tell me how many of you were in the cave?'

'Seven.'

Theodosius studied the tablet some more. 'What were their names?'

Arius held his breath as, one by one, Iamelichos listed off his companions, his strange accent enlivening their names.

'This is very hard to believe,' Theodosius admitted. 'A sleep of three hundred years? How could they survive without food?'

'God knows what needs to be done when he takes responsibility for our affairs,' Iamelichos reminded him. 'He gives the gift of life however he chooses to whomever he chooses.'

'Besides,' interrupted Arius, 'how do you know they were alive? Maybe they died, and God revived them. What does it matter? It is a miracle!'

'It is possible,' Theodosius considered. 'But wouldn't their bodies have decayed if they were left in one position on the rocks?'

Arius shook his head. 'As Excellency Iamelichos said, God knows what he needs to do. Besides, God could have rolled them over now and again.' He turned to Iamelichos. 'Is that not so?'

'I have no idea,' said Iamelichos.

'Excellency,' continued Arius, 'this is the miracle we have been praying for. The dead have been revived! Spirits have been returned to lifeless bodies!'

Iamelichos looked surprised. 'Was this the sign you were searching for? Every night, God takes our souls when we sleep and returns them to our bodies every morning when we awaken. Alas, humans always close their eyes to guidance.'

'But this shall erase any doubt,' insisted Arius. 'God has answered our prayers. He has showed us how he revives the dead.'

'I doubt it,' cautioned Iamelichos. 'Moses and Jesus brought great miracles, and yet people still doubted them.'

Theodosius rose. 'Forget about those who intentionally disbelieve. This miracle will be welcomed by seekers of truth.'

'That is so,' Iamelichos agreed.

'Excellency,' advised Arius, 'we have to return to the cave at once and bring back these holy men. Everyone should witness this miracle.'

Theodosius leaned ponderously on his cane. 'I have a better idea. Order the heralds to spread the news.'

'Now?' asked Arius.

'Yes, now. Tomorrow morning, we will set off for

the cave. Anyone who wishes to sanctify his eyes with the wondrous sign of these holy men may accompany us. Undoubtedly, this is a clear sign ... this is how God breathes life into the dead.'

'It is a great idea,' Arius assured him.

Theodosius nodded. 'Tonight, Excellency Iamelichos may be our guest.'

'Excellency,' Iamelichos requested, 'my friends have been waiting for food since early morning. If we cannot return tonight, can we leave first thing in the morning?'

Theodosius nodded again. 'As you wish. An early start can be arranged.'

A servant then led Iamelichos to the guest chambers – not the same ones Hadrian had slept in, but similar enough. Iamelichos fingered the fringed velveteen draperies. Little seemed to have changed. Would Antonios have been treated with such deference, had he returned in his stead?

The heralds' voices drifted in, shattering the silence of the night. 'The martyrs of the cave have arisen! The martyrs of the cave are alive!'

XXI

REFLECTIONS

Throughout the night, Iamelichos remained awake, immersed in his own thoughts. He was now an individual thrown into a remote era. All his contemporaries, except his companions in the cave, were dead. Time made no sense to him anymore. He had stepped into an era he did not belong to. His small child had died over two hundred fifty years ago, so too his wife. All those he had loved or despised had gone. Maria and Archimedes, Hadrian and Diocletian – how calmly, how silently they had all succumbed!

All the apprehensions and anxieties, all the friendships and enmities, all the torments and intrigues...they had all been subdued by the passage of time, and time had submitted to God. No...time was nothing but the submission of men to God. History was nothing but a record of deaths. Death after death after death. Fifty-some emperors, and only God knew how many governors, commanders, and leaders. And this only within the Roman Empire! Only God knew who had come and gone in other parts of this great world as they had slept. Time was surely a swift stream, its powerful floods washing all away.

All that magnificence and glory, all that pride and conceit – it had all collapsed during one long sleep. A weak and impoverished people whose sole dignity was their ability to bear torture now ruled the whole of the Empire. And all of this during one long sleep! What difference did it make how long the sleep had lasted? To them it had been but a day, or part of a day. And to God, it had not even been a day. A year, a thousand years, a hundred thousand years – to God, all were equal to the blink of an eye.

Iamelichos went to the window. The crescent moon was glittering just as it had three hundred years ago. It was almost dawn. Beneath his window, the officers were busy preparing for the morrow's excursion. They seemed unaware of the passage of time, asleep despite its terrifying sounds. What little time they had, and what abundant desires. How fast they were moving towards annihilation, and how slowly they thought!

He put his head out the window. 'Hey! We have woken up. When do you plan to wake up?'

Fortunately, no one heard him, or else they would have thought him mad.

Returning to the centre of the room, he sat himself upon a finely woven carpet and began to sob without knowing quite why. Was it humility before the power of God? Or his realisation of how God had mysteriously concealed his power in thick shrouds of time? Why should this remain a mystery for all and forever? He saw now that the world was nothing but barren land: whatever planted thereupon would not bear fruit; and, should it bear fruit, it was not worth harvesting.

But only he who had been favoured by God could perceive the deceptiveness of this world and hear its detestable voice. Others were still deaf and blind. Perhaps this was why he was weeping? Mankind indulged in such inebriety, caused such turmoil, and raised such dust so that they would not see themselves in its haze, so they could avoid comprehending the truth of life.

Why does no one understand? Iamelichos lamented. Why does no one see? Why does no one hear? Do we not all have hearts and ears and eyes? Why could I not perceive these things three hundred years ago? How thick this varnish is which can only be erased by death! O World, how smoothly you deceive, and how crudely you delude. Maybe this is the way things need to be; this is the only way human life can continue. Maybe only the elite are meant to understand this.

'Sir!' a servant's voice called in. 'Excellency Theodosius is awaiting you.'

The servant must have been knocking for some time. Raising his head from the floor, he glanced out the window. Morning had arrived without warning. Slowly, he got up and readied himself.

A few minutes later, the caravan of pilgrims set off. At the front, Iamelichos rode in a carriage accompanied by Theodosius, Marius, Arius, and the Bishop. The carriages of other prominent citizens followed behind them, along with a full complement of guards. A swarm of people trailed behind them – some in disbelief, some in amazement, and some in religious exaltation. Unbeknownst to Iamelichos, Filus eagerly walked among them, hopeful that he might perhaps acquire the light of true Christianity from Christians who had lived nearer to the era of Jesus and were innocent of the religious intrigues that had succeeded them.

As they rode, Iamelichos began to preach. 'Excellency Theodosius! You are now the governor of Philadelphia and seated upon a throne which, during our era, was occupied by a man named Diocletian. We fled from Diocletian, and now you want us to return. Thus, certainly you are different from him. You are a Christian. You are one of our brethren; and, therefore, I would like to advise you.'

Theodosius sat upright. It was hard to say what he was thinking.

'Excellency Theodosius! God does not look at our titles. He does not care whether we are called Christians or Jews or something else. Today, I have seen the victory of truth over falsehood. But should the righteous leaders of the faith stop circling the axis of truth and instead make themselves the axis, the turbulent floods of truth will remove them, no matter what they call themselves. At one time, the Christians were righteous, and that truth has become victorious and eliminated falsehood and the leaders of falsehood. But now, some falsehoods

245

have penetrated the true religion of Jesus, and here chime the bells of danger. Now, the Christians must take utmost care. Should the Christian emperors live as the pagan emperors did, they are only trying to deceive God with a name – and no one can ever deceive God. Should the Christians follow the beliefs of the idolaters, then they are idolaters and have only taken the name of Christianity. Truth never reads names. Falsehood has no future, whatever title it chooses. It is we who should constantly be seeking the truth, for truth does not follow any name. Am I clear, Excellency Theodosius?'

Theodosius considered his words. The Bishop and Arius were also silent.

Iamelichos continued. 'God told Joshua: *Verily, I shall appoint a rejected group as the chosen ones.* God chose the Israelites and bestowed his benevolence on them when they were the weakest and most impoverished tribe. God chose them because they were with the truth. But, before long, they turned away from the truth and fought against Jesus. Thus, God cursed them and sewed some of their hearts so tightly that faith could not enter. And now, Excellency Theodosius, God has chosen us. The people of Jesus. Am I making myself clear, Your Excellency?'

'What do you mean?' the Bishop asked tentatively.

'I fear that the Christians have distanced themselves from Jesus, whereas Jesus was not far removed from the truth.' Looked out across the familiar yet unfamiliar lands, he voiced the concern that had been growing in his mind. 'How far till Mount Angelos?'

Arius surveyed the land. 'Not far.'

'My friends are not aware of the passage of this long time,' Iamelichos said. 'Should they see this crowd, they will think I have been arrested, and they are trapped. They might even flee from the cave and seek refuge elsewhere, and we might never see them again.'

'What should be done?' asked Theodosius.

'It is best for me to ride ahead on horseback and inform them of these three hundred years they have lost.'

'Or the three hundred years they have found,' observed Arius sagely.

Minutes later, Iamelichos, mounted on a white mare, distanced himself from the caravan and headed for the cave.

XXII

THE PRAYER

Iamelichos' companions waited uneasily in the cave. Their gnawing hunger had only allowed them to sleep a few hours. After their morning prayers, they had waited wordlessly for Iamelichos to return with bread, or news, or both. Hunger had overwhelmed them.

As Martinos dragged himself over to the entrance, pale sunrays scattered around him. The birds were chirping their morning routine, frustratingly out of reach. He wondered if there was something they could eat in the foliage.

'Nothing is happening,' he reported.

Worry lines creased Maximilian's face. 'Should he not return before noon, we will need to come up with another plan.'

'What if they captured him?' asked Antonios worriedly.

'There is nothing we can do.' The all-too-familiar words echoed off the cave, punctuated by the mountain breeze.

'He never saw Archimedes before he left,' Joannes recalled. 'He probably hid in his own house last night.'

'No,' Maximilian objected sharply. 'All of our houses are being watched. He promised not to contact anyone, and he never breaks his word.'

'I hope he did not have to sleep in the wilderness,' said Antonios. 'It was very cold last night, and he had no food.'

'No colder than the palace barracks,' Maximilian reminded him.

'Imagine if he showed up on the palace doorstep,' laughed Martinos grimly. 'Paid a visit to His Excellency Diocletian.'

Antonios looked down. 'Wherever he is, I hope he comes back soon.'

'Amen,' prayed Maximilian.

Their strength exhausted, their minds wandered back into the dim haze of hunger and sleep.

Listlessly, Joannes traced out invisible shapes onto the cave floor – one for each of his children. He had known, of course, that he would never see them again. But only now had it begun to sink in.

He knew he should be sad. And he did feel sad. But, at the same time, another feeling was interfering with his sadness. He felt as if he had arrived at the fountain of joy. He had placed himself in the hands of God and lost all his sadness. It was amazing. He would not have exchanged a second of this sweetness for anything – not even eternal life.

Wrapping his arms around himself to keep out the cold, Martinos wandered back over to the mouth of the cave. Suddenly, he let out a shout. 'He's coming!'

They scrambled over to the entrance. Indeed, Iamelichos was crunching hastily across the dry leaves.

'It is he, thank God!' rejoiced Antonios.

Suddenly, Dionysios froze. 'Look at the valley!'

An ocean of bronzed carriages had flooded the slopes. Like sinking ships, the carriages were being abandoned at an alarming rate, and the riders were crawling up towards them.

'They must have followed him,' sighed Martinos. 'We never really had any hope.'

Exakoustodianos squinted at the royal carriages. 'Hadrian and Diocletian came for us personally? That's not like them. They always left the dirty work to the soldiers.'

'Unprecedented,' agreed Maximilian. 'And, my God, half of Philadelphia seems to have come too!'

Quietly, Joannes asked, 'What should we do?'

Maximilian drew himself up. 'The same as always. Prepare ourselves for death. I swear to God, I have never been so eager for death. They are all that lie between ourselves and our encounter with God. I am ready to meet my Lord.' Nonchalantly, he sat back down in the cave and began to utter ancient phrases in praise of God. In his eyes now shone a ray of hope.

'I too want to meet my Lord,' confided Joannes. 'But we have to try to find a way out. Antonios, you know this cave best. Can we escape out the other side?'

'We could,' Antonios acknowledged. The teeming masses reminded him of ants swarming fallen crumbs of bread — and they were the crumbs. 'But I believe they know exactly where we are. We had better wait for Excellency Iamelichos. He will know what to do.'

Touched by Antonios' faith, Joannes did not pursue the question any more.

Before long, Iamelichos came running towards the cave. He sank down and caught his breath. He had not brought any food.

Joannes rushed over to him. 'What happened? Didn't you see them? They followed you!'

Iamelichos smiled a mysterious smile. 'Do not fear. They are all your friends.'

Joannes gaped. 'Our friends?'

'Yes,' affirmed Iamelichos. 'They have come to return you to the city in reverence.'

Speechless, they followed him into the cave, whereupon Maximilian immediately rose. 'Ah, dear Iamelichos! Thank God I am seeing you again! I don't know why I missed you so much last night.'

'You should have missed me,' Iamelichos replied cryptically. 'We have been friends for centuries.'

Maximilian looked at him peculiarly. 'Iamelichos? Are you all right? What happened down there?'

Seemingly oblivious to the growing roar of voices outside, Iamelichos smiled freely again. 'None of you can guess how long we have slept.'

'Who cares?' pleaded Martinos. 'They're almost here!'

Iamelichos seemed absolutely radiant. 'God has answered our prayers in a way we can never sufficiently thank him for. We were under attack by evil beliefs, and our hearts shook under the tyranny of falsehood. At such a moment, we entrusted ourselves to God, and God took responsibility for us and granted us life without requiring us to toil for our livelihood.'

'Iamelichos,' begged Martinos. 'What are you talking about?'

Iamelichos faced his bewildered, anxious friends. 'We have slept in this cave for three hundred years.'

They stared at each other in disbelief.

'Hadrian is gone. Diocletian is gone. Christianity rules the Empire. These people outside are descendants of the Philadelphians you once knew, three hundred years removed. They have come to welcome you back from exile.'

Maximilian had never known Iamelichos to lie, not even in jest. And certainly not in a situation like this. 'Are you sure?' he asked.

'Completely,' vowed Iamelichos. 'God has showed us how he holds the world in his omnipotent grasp. He has taught us that time has no meaning. Whatever happens is but the enforcement of his command. His enemies flee from him only to run faster towards him.'

'Praise be to God,' murmured Antonios.

'Time had shrouded these truths from us, but now God has removed the veil of time from our eyes.' His eyes were brimming with understanding. 'Wait, and you will see.'

They had no choice but to wait. By now, the ground was trembling with the onslaught of feet.

An enthusiastic voice called into the cave. 'Excellency Iamelichos!'

Curiously, the six glanced at each other. It didn't sound like one of Diocletian's henchmen. Cautiously, they crept out.

There stood six strange, and yet strangely familiar men.

Theodosius' eyes flickered across the crumbled remnants of the wall. He could have easily passed for Diocletian.

Marius was filling his eyes with the sight of these fabled men whose story he had told and retold. He bore an uncanny resemblance to Iamelichos.

Arius was sketching every stitch of their clothing onto a wax tablet. He seemed perfectly at home with them.

But, tentatively, Father Filus stepped towards them. He bowed, and bowed again.

Ceremoniously, the Bishop proclaimed, 'God has bestowed us with the favour of meeting you, Excellencies.' A prominent metal cross gleamed from his neck.

Gingerly, Arius and Marius followed Filus into the cave. 'Amazing,' whispered Arius. 'If Sanctus had lived to see this.'

Theodosius sank to his knees. He cast his hand over his eyes, as if he might have been weeping.

Cries began filtering in from the crowd. 'Bless us,

sacred men of God! Holy men of God, favour us!'

'They are all Christians?' Maximilian quietly confirmed.

Iamelichos nodded.

'And they have made us their saints,' whispered Joannes.

A human forest had sprouted outside. From near and far, people were pointing and shouting and explaining and crying. Fear had been replaced with wonder.

Father Filus climbed atop a slab of rock – the same slab that the dog was still resting upon. 'O people of Philadelphia!' he called out. His voice could barely be heard over the chaos. 'O people of Philadelphia!'

The crowd silenced as his voice reverberated from the rocks. 'O believers! O disbelievers! God has chosen you above all peoples. He has shown his great sign to you, and he has closed all doors of doubt. Indeed, this is a blessing beyond all blessings. It is a favour beyond all favours, and we can never offer sufficient thanks for it. Now, none can doubt that the Day of Resurrection is real, for he has shown how he brings the dead back to life!'

Tears flowed from the eyes of the faithful, while the sceptics shot each other knowing glances. 'God has warned you, O creatures of God. Prepare yourselves for death! Take provisions from this world, and know that the best provision is piety. I beseech God to place us among those who recognize that this world is not their final abode, those who would never exchange it for eternal life. God has not created us in vain, and he will not abandon us to oblivion.'

As Father Filus jumped down, the clamour resumed.

Iamelichos took his hand. 'May God grant your prayer, brother.'

'I hope so,' he replied.

Iamelichos' friends climbed up onto the rock for a better look. They took in the crowd, the clothes, the accents, and the uproar. The people peered back – some in reverence, others in disbelief.

'We should return to the palace and celebrate this blessing,' Theodosius suggested.

'The palace?' repeated Maximilian, his face filled with deep disgust. They had all assumed they had forever left the palace behind.

Iamelichos nodded sombrely.

'I never thought I would be invited to a palace,' Antonios said softly. 'But now, the world and the worldly just seem so ridiculous. I just want to flee.'

'I say we explore this magic cave further,' suggested Joannes. 'It has to be miraculous. It has been the site of this great miracle.'

Softly, Martinos added, 'I don't think I'm ready to go back.'

Maximilian faced Theodosius. 'We require more time to consider this extraordinary event. With your leave, we would like to remain alone in this cave until nightfall. Once we return, we will have little chance to think.'

'As you wish,' acknowledged Theodosius. 'You are our guests, not our prisoners.' Maximilian looked relieved. 'Father Filus, stay with them tonight. You may escort them to the palace tomorrow.'

Gladly, Filus settled himself back down onto the rock. Absentmindedly, he stroked the dog. The dog was no longer formidable.

A respectful distance away, the guards stood watch – but, this time, to keep the onlookers out, rather than to keep the fugitives in. Although many people had gone home, multitudes still seemed determined to camp out on the mountain.

Iamelichos and his friends returned to the cave. They had forgotten their hunger. They had seen more than they could digest in the past couple hours. A heavy silence filled the cave. Everyone sat silently, deep in wonder and amazement – no, not wonder; it was an awesome, yet mysterious knowledge.

Finally, Joannes dared to blow away the silence. 'Had we lived outside for three hundred years, we would never have recognized what we know now.'

'*Seek refuge in the cave,*' recalled Exakoustodianos. '*Your God will shower his mercy upon you and quell your distress.* I swear, God is the only conqueror in this world, and all others are besieged by him.'

A light shone in Dionysios' eyes. 'I never understood how the prophets were victorious, how Jesus was victorious over his killers. Now I understand.'

'It's still hard to believe it all disappeared without a trace,' continued Joannes. 'The emperors, the troops, the amphitheatres, the temples. I still remember Judah's body, hanging off of his cross.'

'God does not make haste,' said Maximilian. 'This is the secret of wisdom.' He shook his head. 'Ah, time, time! You hide everything behind yourself. You are a preacher who preaches with no words. But who will listen to your sermon?'

Quietly, Iamelichos spoke up. 'The temples have disappeared, but the emperors have not.'

Maximilian looked at him soberly. Slowly, he nodded.

'Friends!' interrupted Joannes. 'I do not wish to live among people again. I do not want to return to the world. I want....' His eyes filled with tears. 'I want to return to my merciful God, the one who took care of me these three centuries.' He looked around the nondescript cave. 'I want to stay here until the end of my days. This cave is my home! It is more luminous than the sun, more expansive than the world.'

'We do not deserve such a kindness from God,' Iamelichos told him gently, trembling slightly. 'The Creator of the entire world has cast his attention on us humble creatures. He has answered our prayers and watched over us. How can we ask anything more? Remember what Jesus told John about eating in Herod's house.'

'What did he say?' asked Antonios.

'Jesus asked: Have you seen a poor man invited to a wealthy man's house to eat bread? John answered: I have eaten bread in Herod's house. Before I knew thee, I used to be a fisherman and sell fish to Herod's family. One day, when he was feasting, I brought him an excellent

257

fish, and he made me stay and eat.

'Jesus said: May God pardon you! How could you eat with the infidels? But tell me, how did you conduct yourself at the table? Did you seek the most honourable place? Did you ask for the best food? Did you speak without being questioned? Did you consider yourself more worthy than others to sit at the table?

'John answered: By God, I did not dare to lift up my eyes. I was a poor fisherman, clad in tattered clothes, sitting among the king's barons. When the king gave me a little piece of flesh, I thought that the world had fallen upon my head, from the greatness of the favour that the king had done unto me. Had the king been one of us, I would have fain served him all the days of my life.

'Jesus said: This world is a house where God invites men to his feast. Everything we receive, we receive from God. Man ought to bear himself with the deepest humility, knowing his own vileness and the greatness of God. Therefore, we cannot ask why this or that was said or done in this world. Rather, we have to hold ourselves to account, for we are unworthy to stand before God's table. Even the smallest bounty obliges us to spend our entire life for the love of God. As God liveth, you sinned not, John, in eating with Herod, for it was God's will that you did so, in order that you might teach us and everyone that fears God.' Iamelichos fell silent.

'We have eaten with Herod,' murmured Exakoustodianos.

'We had no choice,' said Maximilian.

'And we have become a lesson,' added Iamelichos.

Outside, the guards were yelling. The roar seemed to have escalated.

'Do you think they understand?' asked Dionysios.

Iamelichos lowered his voice. 'Do you remember what Jesus prayed when the people began to follow him in droves?'

'What did he say?' asked Antonios.

'O God, take me from this world, for its inhabitants have become crazed, and they have come close to calling me God.'

They looked at one another, recognition in their eyes.

Quietly, Iamelichos rose and secluded himself in his corner of the cave, the one he had always prayed in. He began to recite the same beautiful words that had drawn Antonios towards him three centuries earlier.

Maximilian put his head in his hands. Throngs of people were ready to return him to the palace where a high priest who now wore a cross awaited with open arms. *They are all that lie between ourselves and God – only now, they are not going to bring us to him. They are going to take us away from him.*

Joannes remembered how peaceful the cave had been the night before. It was the first time he had truly been able to fill his heart with nothing but God. How could their hearts which had been ripped apart for God endure the sombreness of life? How could eagles who had soared the skies again choose the earth for their abode?

One by one, they laid their foreheads on the ground and prayed.

What were they whispering? What were they seeking from God? No one knows. They could have been seeking God's help. They could have been seeking his forgiveness. But, most likely, they were seeking nothing at all. Most likely, they wanted nothing more than to partake in the delight of speaking with God.

As the sweetness of their supplication filled their beings, they lost all thought of the crowds, or the palace, or their hunger, or their families. Outside, the pale sunrays began to dwindle, until afternoon passed seamlessly into evening in the cave.

None of them spoke again.

XXIII

THE STORY

F ather Filus waited on the increasingly uncomfortable rock slab outside the cave. What could they be doing all this time? For a while, he thought he heard them talking, but then their voices petered out. He squinted into the semi-lit cave. The afternoon rays shone askance on it, barely illuminating Iamelichos' form. Iamelichos had touched his forehead to the ground. He remained like that until the sun no longer shone on him at all.

Father Filus was dying to join them, to partake of their luminous spiritual fountain. These men were the divine gift he had been praying for, and he had a thousand questions to ask. Still, he could not bring himself to interrupt their intense spiritual communion. They would emerge soon enough, and he could ask his questions then.

A few soldiers, backs bent, trudged up the mountain. They were lugging sacks of almost-fresh bread, cured

THE IDOLS WILL FALL

olives, and local fruits as well as a gargantuan terra cotta pot steaming with a savoury aroma. Filus peeked inside. It was fresh chicken stew — a delicacy in these regions. The soldiers must have hauled the chicken up from the village and cooked it on one of their fires.

A familiar scent tinged his nostrils, and he shrunk back in disgust. The chicken had been stewed with bacon.

Another soldier was dutifully emptying a wineskin into a water jug he had lugged from a mountain stream. The pure water had clouded into a pale burgundy.

'What are you doing?' demanded Filus.

The soldier nodded towards the cave. 'For the guests.'

'Just give them water,' Filus commanded.

The soldier looked at him strangely. Plain water was for the poor. Holding his tongue, he dragged away the wineskins he had hauled up the mountain. As soon as he reached the groves, he took a couple swigs.

Filus was almost certain that the men of the cave followed the ancient religious law. No pork, no wine. Of course, he had not actually had the chance to ask — but religious law ranked high on his list of questions for them. However, he couldn't believe the cook had been so negligent. What ignorance had come over his people.

Anyway, the chicken stew itself was no matter. Filus hardly expected these men to demand meats. They would prefer the fruits of the earth.

The hearty scent of the crusty bread called to his hungry stomach, but he decided to wait for the men to complete their prayers so they could break bread together. It would be an unparalleled honour.

The afternoon wore on, and he waited impatiently on the rock. How long were they planning to pray?

Absentmindedly, he rested his hand on Comteri. He had developed quite an affection for the three hundred year old dog.

Suddenly, he snapped his hand back. Comteri was cold.

Delicately, he pushed open the dog's eyelids. The dog's eyes stared blankly back at him. The dog was not asleep this time. The dog was dead.

At once, the whole world seemed to fall apart around him. Forgetting his hesitation, he called out, 'Excellency Iamelichos! Excellency Iamelichos!'

There was no response, and he rushed into the cave. In an eerie copy of Iamelichos, all the men had pressed their foreheads to the ground. They were absolutely still, just as they had been when they were sleeping.

'Excellency Iamelichos!' he repeated desperately. 'Holy men of God!'

Had they gone back to sleep? Painstakingly, he crept over to Iamelichos, so as not to disturb him. Iamelichos did not seem to be breathing. Had they been breathing when they were asleep? Gingerly, he rolled Iamelichos over onto his side, apologizing, 'You'll sleep better that way.' Iamelichos' arms and legs protruded unnaturally, so he straightened them and then shrunk back from his handiwork. Iamelichos now looked like a corpse.

Kneeling by his side, Filus gazed forlornly at his

silent companion. Something seemed terribly wrong. Suddenly, he remembered. The fear. For generations, the bravest men had not been able to venture into the cave. How could he just sit here?

Hesitantly, he laid his head on Iamelichos' heart. There was no heartbeat.

Iamelichos was dead – really and truly dead.

Tears streamed from his eyes onto Iamelichos' limp body. He had only met Iamelichos the day before, but he felt as if he had known him for ages. He felt as if he had lost his own brother, his own soul.

In his heart, he knew the others were gone as well. Methodically, he went around and, one by one, laid them to rest. He did not even know who was who. Then, helplessly, he sat down cross-legged on the stone platform and surveyed the seven corpses. All his pent-up frustration came out in wracking sobs. Why had God revived them only to take them away again?

'They were supposed to be a sign,' he lamented to the cave. 'The sign to end all doubt.' He lifted his eyes up to the dank ceiling. 'God, if you meant them to be your sign, bring them back.'

He waited expectantly for the men to rise up from their eternal sleep.

Nothing happened. The cave was absolutely still except for a faint drip in the distance. It seemed to be weeping with him.

Wiping his tears, he filled his eyes with their holy faces. They seemed to be truly at rest, more so than any other of his departed brethren. He almost envied them.

They would not have to face the priesthood, or the palace, or the people. They had gone on to a better place. Indeed, what would have been left for them in this world? They had already achieved the highest human goal. They had reached their Lord, and so they had no need for riches or entertainment. The world would have been naught but a prison.

Curse his shyness. If only he had asked them his questions earlier. But perhaps he was not meant to hear the answers from them. Perhaps he was meant to find them in his own time.

Abruptly, he began to laugh – a bitter, yet hopeful laugh. 'Ah, Filus how ridiculous! Ah, Filus, what a grand lesson! How difficult it is to understand God's signs ... and yet, how simple!'

Still laughing, he left the cave. 'Sir,' he informed the commander, 'they are dead.'

The commander stared at him in horror. 'What?'

'They are dead,' Filus repeated. 'These holy men are dead.' The more he said it, the more it made sense. 'Inform Excellency Theodosius. The awakened have died. The awakened have died.'

Onlookers began pouring out from the groves. Quickly, the soldiers tightened their perimeter, and a few of them drew their swords.

Panicked, the commander sped up to the cave. Soon, he came back down the way he had come. 'Keep them out!' he called breathlessly as he sprinted down to Raqim.

Night fell, and the soldiers were still on alert. Filus

lay down next to the cave. A stream of ants was crawling past him into the victuals left uselessly on the rock. He had not eaten all day, but he had no appetite for food.

He drifted off. In his mind's eye, he saw Iamelichos in his ornate, ancient robes beckoning to him. He ran after him, but Iamelichos disappeared too fast. Then, the scene shifted. They were in the throne room in the palace, and Theodosius was holding a golden sceptre above the pagans who were bickering all around him.

Blinking, he realized it was early morning, and Marius was shaking him. He sat up. 'You heard the news,' he mumbled half-coherently.

Marius nodded grimly.

The grey-bearded palace physician had also trekked up the slopes. Wielding an oversized bag of herbs and implements, he examined the bodies one by one and officially pronounced them dead.

Exhaling deeply, Theodosius stared into the trees, where the morning birds twittered, oblivious to his distress. 'A sleep of three hundred years,' he pondered, and 'one day of wakefulness. I fail to understand God's ways.'

'It is clear, Excellency, most clear,' swore Filus. 'As clear as the sun.'

'I hope so,' murmured Theodosius. He turned to the Bishop. 'What should be done?'

'They must be buried,' the Bishop advised. Filus could tell that was not the answer Theodosius had wanted.

Theodosius leaned heavily on his oaken cane. 'Be it

so. Dig seven graves.'

'Eight graves,' interrupted Filus.

Theodosius raised his eyebrows. 'Eight?'

'The dog,' Filus explained. One of the palace advisors hastily stifled a chortle. 'The dog was not worth less than a human.' He shot a glance at the advisor. 'It was worth more than many humans. What it must have done to have merited such an honour.'

'Very well,' Theodosius acceded. 'Eight graves.'

As the soldiers hoisted their picks and shovels into the cave, Marius sank down next to Filus on the rock. 'I wish I hadn't gone home yesterday.'

Filus rested his hand on his shoulder comfortingly. 'You didn't know. None of us thought this would happen.' His face suddenly shone. 'It was beautiful, the way they passed on. Nothing could have interrupted their prayers. God took them when they were closest to him.'

Marius half-smiled. 'We should be so fortunate.'

Suddenly, an idea struck Filus. 'We should build a house of worship over them to keep their memory alive.'

Marius did not need to be asked twice. With renewed energy, he sprung up from the rock and examined the edifice. 'It's like a natural shelf. It wouldn't be too hard to build a church up there.'

'And there's plenty of wood,' observed Filus.

Together, they approached Theodosius, who was sitting alone, a troubled look on his face.

'Excellency,' Filus suggested, 'generations to come will be making pilgrimages to this holy place, this site of

God's great sign. How about constructing a church here?'

Theodosius nodded slowly. 'Not a bad idea.'

Frowning, one of his advisors stepped forward. His name was Heraclius, and his pagan name suited his pagan outlook. 'Excellency,' he objected, 'are you really planning to elevate uncivilized cavemen?'

Filus could not believe his ears. 'Uncivilized cavemen?'

Heraclius glared at him. This was hardly their first difference of opinion. 'How do you know what they were doing in that cave? Did you see them?' He gestured out at the greenery around him. 'Maybe they were just long lived. The mountain air is quite healthy, and they could have subsisted quite comfortably on berries and venison.'

'They don't have a grey hair on their heads,' countered Filus, 'and you are telling me they are three hundred years old?'

'So what?' retorted Heraclius. 'Everyone else thought they were dead — even Marius. Why cling to the quaint notion they were asleep?'

Filus stared at him in speechless astonishment while Marius hung his head in his hands.

'Even if they were asleep,' Heraclius continued, 'what kind of accomplishment is that?'

Marius flushed. Quickly, Heraclius ameliorated, 'Do not misunderstand. I'm not accusing them of lying. I'm just saying we don't know. No one else has ever slept for three hundred years ... have they?'

'It is a sign from God,' Filus growled. 'A miracle. A sign.' Somehow, he didn't think Heraclius would be able to get that into his thick head.

'Oh, yes, the common folk love signs,' Heraclius derided him. 'We should know better. We should not pay homage to men who are centuries removed from modern civilization. Roman civilization arrived here only recently. We do not want to go backward.'

'No worries about that,' muttered Filus.

Heraclius glowered. 'Honestly, I do not understand all this business about a sign. What does the afterlife have to do with a bunch of old corpses?'

Filus could not restrain himself any longer. 'Since when have you ever seen a three hundred year old corpse? Or maybe you don't believe they were three hundred years old. Maybe they weren't really Diocletian's counsellors. Maybe Diocletian didn't have any counsellors. Maybe he didn't even exist. Maybe the historians were all just big liars, conspiring to take Philadelphia back to the dark ages.'

'Watch your words,' Heraclius warned him.

Filus ignored him. 'A pity that God's mysteries enter your soul through your eyes. You limit the world to what you see, and, the one time you actually see the truth, you deny it. Should you and the likes of you see a thousand signs, you would never believe. You are a failure, Heraclius. A failure of humanity. These men have succeeded, and you have failed.'

Heraclius raised his hand as if he were about to strike Filus.

'Enough,' Theodosius intervened. He sounded tired. 'We will build a church here.'

'Excellency — ' interrupted Heraclius angrily.

Theodosius silenced him with his eyes. 'As far as I am concerned, it was a sign.' He turned to Filus. 'After you have prepared the corpses for burial, allow the people to view them. But make sure they don't touch them. You know this lot. They'll rip their shrouds to pieces for benediction.'

Filus and Marius nodded. Heraclius still looked livid.

With no further comment, Theodosius turned and struggled down the slopes. A couple soldiers rushed to his aid, but he waved them off and eased his descent with his cane.

Marius was still staring at the ground.

'You should be ashamed of yourself,' Filus reprimanded Heraclius. 'You dare to speak of the departed like this.'

Glaring, Heraclius stomped away. Soon, he was running after Theodosius.

Filus settled back down next to Marius. 'Iamelichos warned us,' he recalled. 'He predicted they would not believe. At first, I didn't believe him.'

Marius lifted his head.

'I always wondered how Jesus' people could deny him,' Filus continued. 'I mean, he raised the dead. Now I understand.'

Marius nodded. 'It has always been like this.'

They sat in silence for a while. Finally, Marius said

grimly, 'Let's prepare the corpses.'

As they carried the shrouds into the cave, Marius took one last glimpse at his ancestor's face. 'Hail and farewell,' he murmured, before they began the shrouding. It was hard work. Finally, the soldiers lowered their guard, and the expectant masses pressed towards the cave like water bursting through a dam. As they came and went, each person seemed changed – but each in a different way. Some were tearful. Others were thoughtful. Some were speechless, and a few were sniggering. It was amazing how everyone saw the sign so many different ways – as if the sign really revealed what was inside themselves. It was as if their eyes could only see what was inside themselves, not what was outside.

As quickly as it had sprouted, the human forest disappeared. No longer needed, the guards broke camp. After paying his final respects, even Marius headed home. However, Filus could not tear himself away from the cave. Unbidden, his heart prayed that he could join them in their eternal journey.

It was not meant to be. He still had tasks to complete in this world. But he knew that, before long, he would be following in Iamelichos' footsteps and spending long nights secluded in the mysterious cave.

Alone, he walked over to the groves, pebbles crunching under his feet. Suddenly, he roared, 'Why are these people blind?'

His voice carried throughout the valley, and a couple curious stragglers turned back before continuing on their way.

They would tell their friends, and their neighbours, and their children, and their children's children, but the story of the seven sleepers would only be that – a story. The people could not see.

Disillusioned, Filus returned to the cave. The men's long slumber was seeming less and less strange. What befuddled him was how these people were asleep – how, for millennia, all but the faithful had willingly put themselves into a deep sleep and refused to awaken at any call.

Dipping down towards the horizon, the sun shone blood red through the pine trees. 'Why do you keep coming back?' he asked it. 'Why do you keep pouring your rays on these heedless people?' He sighed. 'Perhaps you hope to return tomorrow and shine upon a people who understand the meaning of life. Yes, perhaps you were created for them, not for these uninvited guests.'

A cool breeze began to blow. 'Three hundred years...so much you have witnessed,' Filus called after the disappearing sun. 'Love and hate, praise and thanklessness, imprisonment and tyranny, defeat and victory. So many stories you could tell! But have you ever seen a beggar who remained a beggar? Have you ever seen a king who remained a king? Have you ever seen a people who endured?'

Stretching himself out on the damp ground, he spent the next night out in the open beside the cave.

The next morning, the sun predictably raised her head from the east and graced the people of Philadelphia with her life-giving rays. Life returned to normal. The priests went to their churches, and the moneylenders went to their stores. The merchants sold their wares, and the advisors returned to the palace. The miraculous happenings eventually faded back into the fabric of everyday life. All that remained was a story of the seven sleepers in the cave.

POSTSCRIPT

The story you have just read is based on a narration in the Holy Qur'an in the chapter entitled *The Cave*.[1]

> Do you suppose that the Companions of the Cave and the Raqim were among our signs, a wonder? When the youths took refuge in the Cave and they said, 'Our Lord! Grant us a mercy from yourself, and help us on to rectitude in our affair.' So we put them to sleep in the Cave for a number of years. Then we awakened them that we might know which of the two groups better reckoned the period they had stayed.

> We relate to you their account in truth. They were indeed youths who had faith in their Lord, and we had enhanced them in guidance. And we

[1] Qur'an, 18:9-26, slightly adapted from the translation by Ali Quli Qara'i (2004), *The Qur'an, With a Phrase-by-Phrase English Translation*, London: ICAS Press.

fortified their hearts, when they stood up and said, 'Our Lord is the Lord of the heavens and the earth. We will never invoke any god besides Him, for then we shall certainly have said an atrocious lie. These—our people—have taken gods besides Him. Why do they not bring any clear authority touching them? So who is a greater wrongdoer than he who fabricates a lie against God? And as you have dissociated yourselves from them and from what they worship except God, then take refuge in the Cave. Your Lord will unfold His mercy for you, and He will help you on to ease in your affair.'

You may see the sun, when it rises, slanting toward the right of their cave, and, when it sets, cut across them towards the left, while they are in a cavern within it. That is one of God's signs. Whomever God guides is rightly guided, and whomever He leads astray, you will never find for him any guardian or guide. You will suppose them to be awake, although they are asleep. We turn them to the right and to the left, and their dog [lies] stretching its forelegs at the threshold. If you come upon them, you will surely turn to flee from them, and you will surely be filled with a terror of them.

So it was that we awakened them so that they might question one another. One of them said, 'How long have you stayed [here]?' They said, 'We have stayed a day, or part of a day.' They said, 'Your Lord knows best how long you have stayed. Send one of you to the city with this money. Let him observe which of them has the purest food, and bring you provisions from there. Let him be careful and let him not make anyone aware of you. Indeed should they prevail over you, they will [either] stone you [to death], or force you back into their creed, and then you will never be saved.' So it was that We let them come upon them, that they might know that God's promise is true, and that there is no doubt in the Hour. As they were disputing among themselves about their matter, they said, 'Build a building over them. Their Lord knows them best.' Those who had the say in their matter said, 'We will set up a place of worship over them.'

They will say, '[They are] three; their dog is the fourth of them, or they will say, '[They are] five, their dog is the sixth of them,' taking a shot at the invisible [with a wild guess]. And they will say, '[They are] seven, their dog is the eighth of them.' Say, 'My Lord knows best their number, and none knows them except a few.' So do not dispute concerning them, except for a seeming dispute, and do not question about any of them.

Do not say about anything, 'I will indeed do it tomorrow,' Without [adding], 'if God wishes.' And when you forget, remember your Lord, and say, 'Maybe my Lord will guide me to [something] more akin to rectitude than this.' They remained in the Cave for three hundred years, and added nine more [to that number]. Say, 'God knows best how long they remained. To Him belongs the Unseen of the heavens and the earth. How well does He see! How well does He hear! They have no guardian besides Him, and none shares with Him in His judgment.'

These verses only relate the essentials of the story and not the minute historical details that would distract from the moral message of the allegory. For instance, neither the men's names nor their city is mentioned. However, narrations from the Prophet (S) with details about the men of the cave have been recorded in both Sunni and Shi'a collections; relevant works would include *Al-Durr al-Manthur* (Al-Suyuti), *Bihar al-Anwar* ('Allamah Majlisi), *Tafsir al-Burhan* (Sayyid Hashim Bahrani), and the *tafsir* by Abu al-Futuh Razi).[2] This story has also been mentioned by Christian historians, the first of whom was Jacques de Saroug (d. 521 AD) who wrote in Syriac. Local legends and archaeological evidence also hint at details of this story.

However, many of these accounts are contradictory. Even within the Islamic sources, there is no consensus on the men's location, occupation, social status, era, or even religion (although the fact that Christian historians have related the story supports the narrations that the men were Christian). Although the Holy Qur'an connects the men to Raqim, accounts differ as to what Raqim was, with some accounts suggesting it was a town; others, a desert; and, still others, a stone plaque. The historical accounts also differ regarding the era these men lived in; in this regard, the view of Jacques de Saroug has been taken — namely, that the men awakened sometime between 435 and 439 AD. Some Islamic narrations relate that the men lived under the rule of Diocletian, and this book was written under the premise

---

[2] For a detailed analysis of the varying accounts of the seven sleepers, see the commentary of these verses in *Tafsir al-Mizan* by 'Allamah Tabataba'i.

that Diocletian was the name of their local ruler, rather than the Roman Emperor.

Geographically speaking, the Qur'anic verses only indicate that the cave faced south and that a house of worship was built upon it. Historians have suggested Ephesus, Tarsus, Damascus, Palestine, and Philadelphia (modern-day Amman, Jordan) as the location of the cave. Additionally, local legends in Damascus, Palestine, Caucasia, and even Scandanavia identify caves that the men could have slept in. However, the most compelling evidence placing the men in Philadelphia is the discovery of a cave in 1976 about eight miles out of Amman.[3] The remains of seven humans and one dog were found in this cave as well as faded Arabic and Greek inscriptions and an etching of a dog. This cave happens to be located near the present-day village of Rajib, which could easily have been the original village of Raqim. Additionally, the remains of a Byzantine monastery were found on the site; with the advent of Islam, the monastery was converted to a mosque, and remains of the mosque are also present. This evidence, in addition to the historical accounts, has led to the story being placed in Philadelphia.

While the Qur'anic verses do not contain many explicit details, certain aspects of the story may be inferred from them. For instance, since the verses refer

---

[3] Reported in the Egyptian newspaper *Al-Ahram* in 1976. Details of the cave are also mentioned by 'Allamah Tabataba'i in *Tafsir al-Mizan* in the commentary on these verses.

to 'the cave' rather than 'a cave', Iamelichos was assumed to have frequented the cave before their sleep. Similarly, since, according to the verses, the men flee first and then take refuge in the cave, it was assumed that the men travelled first to Raqim and then to the cave. The age of the men was taken from the description of them being 'youths'. Additionally, it should be noted that while the Qur'an relates that the men slept for 309 years, the Qur'an was initially presented to a society that used a lunar calendar, and 309 lunar years is the equivalent of 300 solar years.

However, given the uncertainties in the accounts, a certain amount of intelligent guesswork was necessary to construct a fluid historical account. The details of the story, such as the descriptions and the dialogue, should not be taken as factual; rather, they should be taken as an interpretation of what might have happened. Nonetheless, the main structure and themes of the story should reflect the Qur'anic narrative. Rein of imagination is only permissible to the point where it does not override realities; rather, it should be a mirror for reflecting them. Using these details, I tried to reflect the exalted character of the men and the baseness of their people

Throughout the book, Jesus and the Old Testament prophets have been quoted. Some of these quotations come from the Holy Qur'an and Islamic sources, while others come from the Bible. Portions of the apocryphal Gospel of Barnabas have also been included. Historical details were taken from commonly accepted Roman historical sources.

I am writing this endnote while the translator of this work, Houri Sanizadeh, is no longer among us. She passed away a couple of months ago after a long and brave battle against a malignant disease. While I express my feelings of both grief and gratitude, I am sure the publication of this book will mean a lot to her soul and to her family. I would also like to abundantly thank the editor, Amina Inloes. She not only edited and proofread the book, but also added much beauty and value to it by her additions and omissions and by her literary artwork that gave the whole text more life and attraction.

Finally, I have to say that this pen has been set on paper in all humility in the hope of the magnanimity of the readers, and the rest is left to guidance. If the work is faulty, it is only natural; if it is graced with success, it is but through the grace of God.

Muhammad Saeed Bahmanpour
April 2009

EDITOR'S NOTE

This work was originally published in Persian and has been translated into English. After translation, significant changes were made to the original text. The setting and characters were elaborated on to improve the readability for an English-speaking audience not assumed to be familiar with ancient times. Additionally, some of the dialogue in this version was not present in the original work, and portions of the original work were also omitted for the sake of brevity. Therefore, while every attempt has been made to preserve the spirit and intent of the original work as well as the sanctity of the main characters, this work should be seen as an adaptation based on the original rather than as a faithful translation.

A screenplay of the original story has been produced in Iran under the title *Mardan-e-Anjelos* and is available with English subtitles. It was written by the author, M.S. Bahmanpour.

Amina Inloes
April 2009